D1276582

HOME TO TEXAS

HOME TO TEXAS

TODHUNTER BALLARD

Mishawaka-Penn-Harris
Public Library
Mishawaka, Indiana

Sagebrush
Large Print Westerns

First published in the United States by Doubleday

First published in Great Britain by Hale

Published in Large Print 2005 by ISIS Publishing Ltd,
7 Centremead, Osney Mead, Oxford OX2 0ES,
United Kingdom
by arrangement with
Golden West Literary Agency

British Library Cataloguing in Publication Data
Ballard, Todhunter, 1903–
    Home to Texas. – Large print ed. –
    (Sagebrush western series)
    1. Western stories
    2. Large type books
    I. Title
    813.5'2 [F]

ISBN 0–7531–7287–9 (hb)

Printed and bound by Antony Rowe, Chippenham

CHAPTER
ONE

From his spot in the sheltering brush beside the trail Dork Wallace watched the single rider moving forward toward the riverbank. At this point the Rio Grande was hardly deeper than a trickle below a horse's knees.

The rider meant to cross. If he only intended to water his animal he would not have splashed to the middle of the stream. He was too far away to see a face but from the high crowned hat and bright serape Wallace took him to be Mexican.

That he was alone stirred Dork's curiosity. The border had been restless for months. Apaches had raided back and forth, sweeping from southern Arizona Territory clear into the Big Bend country of Texas. Unless he was very aware of Apache ways no rider was safe venturing alone into the valley, yet whoever was walking the horse through the last of the water was taking no precaution at all to conceal his presence.

The horse lurched up the shelving bank and the rider curbed it, turned and waved as if in farewell to someone hidden behind the low hills on the southern side. Then he faced north again and climbed the small draw directly toward where Wallace stood beside his animal, came over the little hump between them and abruptly reined in when he saw Dork watching him.

There was a rifle in the boot under the rider's knee and a small revolver at his hip. His hand dropped to the ivory stock above the holster.

"Who are you? What do you want?"

Wallace started. He still could not see much of the face between the low drawn hat brim and the red handkerchief over the nose for protection from dust, but there was no mistaking the voice. The rider was a woman.

She spoke English but the accent was Spanish. Recovering, Wallace took off his hat.

"I'm looking for a bunch of cattle some bandits stole from my boss."

Without hesitation she said, "They are twenty-five miles into Mexico. I passed them four hours ago, Rojas' men."

"You know them?"

Her shrug was sharp. "Everyone in northern Coahuila knows Pedro Rojas and his gang. We should." Her voice turned bitter. "There is hardly a family where men have not been murdered and women raped by those jackals."

Dork Wallace had long heard of the outlaw but never come into direct contact with him, and he asked in suspicion, "How did you get away from them?"

"They didn't see me. I saw the dust the drive was making and hid in a coulee until they passed."

He said, "You shouldn't be riding alone here. Chato's Apaches are out."

Again she lifted her shoulder. "I haven't any choice."

She did not sound concerned, pulling down the handkerchief and disclosing a young mouth, then taking off the hat, wiping an arm across her forehead. Wallace had another surprise. She was a golden blonde and the eyes that had been shadowed were revealed as deep blue-gray.

"You . . . aren't Mexican?"

"I was raised in Mexico."

"But you're American?"

Another shrug said it was not important. "My parents were, until they emigrated after the war."

He understood then. A lot of Southerners had moved south after the ruinous defeat. He said, "Do they know you're out here by yourself?"

"They are dead. Rojas raided our ranch, drove off our peons, and rounded up our cattle. My father and mother forted up in the hacienda but it did no good." The voice was toneless, without feeling, as if all emotion had been crushed out of her. "I was visiting in Chihuahua City. When I got home the place was burned. The cattle were gone. There was nothing left, nothing to stay for."

Wallace said, "How long since you've eaten?"

"Yesterday sometime. I found some corn and parched it."

Wallace turned to his horse for the tote sack he had tied behind the saddle just before he discovered the rider across the river. He built up the little fire again, put his blackened coffeepot back on the rocks, sliced bacon into the frying pan, and dropped his leftover sour dough biscuits on the meat to warm.

From the corner of his eye he saw her dismount cautiously and stay close to her horse until the coffee boiled. He poured his cup full, carried it to a rock ten feet away and left it there. When he went back to turn the bacon she walked to the rock and sat down, drinking the hot liquid greedily. On her feet Wallace saw that she was tall, perhaps five-ten, long legged in black riding breeches and boots.

The bacon was done. He took the pan to her with a pointed stick to lift the meat and watched as she ate it and turned the biscuits in the hot grease and chewed them, wolfing in her hunger. He had eaten half an hour before but it made him hungry again to watch her.

He did not distract her with questions until she had wiped the skillet clean and licked her fingers for the last of the grease, then he said, "You have relatives?"

"You might call him that. There's an uncle. If he's still alive."

"You mean to stay with him?"

She was silent, looking into Wallace's face with a direct, hard stare and her chin tightened. Then she burst out savagely.

"I am going to take the ranch away from him."

Wallace started. "Take . . . his ranch . . . ?"

"It isn't his. It's mine."

"How's that?"

The flare changed to dull, tired anger. "When my father decided to go to Mexico after the war he left the ranch for his brother to sell. He was supposed to invest

4

whatever he got for it in cattle and drive them down to our new place in Chihuahua. Instead he kept it and ran it as his own."

"Did your father deed it to him?"

"No. Only gave him a power of attorney to negotiate the sale."

"Why didn't your father go back and sell it himself?"

"He couldn't. Because on our way to Mexico some federal troops tried to stop us. My father killed two of them, one a negro sergeant, one a white officer. He was indicted for murder. If he came north of the line he would be hanged."

Wallace put a handful of greasewood on the embers and set the coffeepot to heat again. "What do you think you can do?"

"Find me a lawyer, a smart lawyer. Daddy always said if a lawyer was smart enough he could get away with anything. Including murder."

Wallace said nothing. She studied him thoughtfully and asked abruptly, "You work for a ranch, you said?"

"I'm a foreman."

"How much do you make?"

He was taken aback. It was none of her business and he was deliberately close-mouthed about his wages. The men under him made twenty a month and found. If they learned he drew a hundred there might be jealousy and trouble. But he reasoned that this girl would not likely be talking with the riders on his employer's spread.

"A hundred and found." He said it slowly.

"American?"

5

He nodded.

"That's a lot these days. You must be very good." She used a feminine guile. "I think only one of the best foremen in south Texas would get so much."

He laughed in embarrassment. "You might tell old man Pease that. My boss. He usually points out my shortcomings with every four letter word in the book."

She showed a quick interest. "You don't get along with him?"

Wallace raised his brows and poked at the fire. Nobody could get along with old Frank Ace Pease. He was into an irascibility as wicked as an angry rattlesnake's and he loved to argue. Pease had come ashore on Galvaston Island as a ten-year-old cabin boy from one of the New England coasters that put in for tallow from the factory and for the cured hides that littered the beach in humpback piles. He had hidden until the little ship spread sail and headed for New Orleans, then he had come out and talked Hank Johns into hiring him at the factory where he scraped hair off the rotting hides and generally made himself useful.

It had been a hard school. With never enough to eat he had grown to barely five feet, but that was all rawhide. He had hazed the cattle gone wild during the war out of the thorny brush and kicked them up the trail to start a ranch. At sixty-five he could outride, outshoot, outshout, and outcurse any of the crew. And in the years between he had spread out across Texas until no one could say how many acres he controlled or how many cattle wore the Lazy P brand.

"We manage," Dork said. "He fires me a couple of times a year just to keep in practice. First time, I loaded my gear and hi-tailed for Del Rio. Next day he came after me. Now I just leave my bedroll in the bunkhouse and light for Fox Corners and the nearest saloon. A couple of days and I ride back and take over like nothing happened."

She did not smile. "You wouldn't have that trouble if you'd come to work for me."

She was as full of surprises as the dregs of a whiskey keg. "Doing what?"

"Helping get my ranch for me, then running it."

He looked her over curiously and said, "You'd hire a man you don't even know his name? He don't know yours?"

"I am Ann Royer . . . Mister . . ."

Again she startled him. "Royer . . . Your uncle doesn't happen to be Phil Royer?"

"He is. You know him?"

"I carry a shot from his gun. It's too close to a main artery for the doc to take it out."

Her eyes lighted with triumph. "Then this is your chance to get back at him."

Dork Wallace laughed. She was like a cat jumping its prey. "I've got no cause to get back, Miss Royer. He wasn't shooting at me on purpose. He and my boss were arguing over a drift fence and he pulled a gun on Pease. I tried to take it away from him and it went off between us. I don't really blame him because Pease was in the wrong. I'm sorry, ma'am, but my job will do as is."

She chewed her lip awhile, then stood up. "I don't understand you," she told him, walked away and mounted.

He watched her go without looking back. When she was out of sight he dumped the coffee on the fire, packed his tote bag and rode.

"And I don't envy Phil Royer." He said it aloud to his horse. "I'd say he's got a vixen on his back. A regular hell-cat from the looks of her."

CHAPTER
TWO

Ace Pease's lasting pleasure was to stand in the breezeway of his Texas house and gaze across the curving valley toward the cottonwoods bordering the serpentine course of sluggish Newmark Creek.

The sun was nearly down. The afternoon heat still shimmered in the quiet air. The horizons wavered. No breath moved by him. He had built this place nearly fifty years ago; at least he had built the cabin that was now the cookshack and grub room for the crew. Later he had added the second cabin and connected it with the first by a roofed-over passage locally known as the trot. There were a thousand houses like it across the West for wherever the Texans had taken their trail herds they had also taken the same architecture.

Old man Pease had built new barns, a blacksmith shop, quarters for his increasing crew as his wealth grew, but it had never occurred to him to build a better house. He lived alone in the two-room cabin, his quarters littered with guns, broken spurs, and worn out hats, for he never threw anything away no matter how shabby it became. But he took an immense pride in the fact that in whatever direction he looked every single mile and acre he could see belonged to him.

He turned slowly, pivoting on his small feet, stopping when he saw the rider small against the distant trees. It was probably Dork Wallace coming back empty-handed to say the missing cows had been run into Mexico. His small, thin-lipped mouth turned down. The thought that even Pedro Rojas would dare strike at the Lazy P was intolerable. He was tempted to mount the crew and ride across the border and give the bandit a lesson. But they had a long head start and it would take time when there was work here to be done. Ace Pease begrudged time almost as much as he begrudged money.

As the rider came closer he decided it was not Dork Wallace. The figure did not sit loose and giving with the rhythm that characterized his foreman. But he did not know it was a girl until she came through the gate into the ranch yard proper.

Now another rider appeared, coming behind her, and that was Dork. Pease came out of the breezeway, down the step to the grit and reached the corner of the big corral just as the girl pulled her horse to the pole fence and stepped down.

Pease noted with an expert eye that the animal had been hard ridden, unconsciously glanced at the brand and found it unfamiliar. He had been too long in the country to show any reaction to the unexpected. He planted himself, blocking the path to the house.

"Come far?"

She was tying the rein to the fence. "From Chihuahua."

That was a long ride. Pease looked from the girl to Wallace as he came through the gate, then back to the visitor.

"Going far?"

She shrugged. "Del Rio, I guess. I have to find a place to stay."

"Come a mite out of your way. Quicker to follow down the river."

"I want a look at the Royer place. Is this it?"

"No ma'am. This here's Lazy P. Phil Royer is about ten miles east. You a friend of Phil's?"

She stretched to her full height with her chin up. "He's my uncle and a thief. He stole our ranch from my father."

Pease's eyes brightened like small dark, damp licorice drops. "Stole it how?"

She told him the story she had told Wallace and Pease's interest came alive.

"You come to try to get it back?"

"As soon as I can recruit a crew, yes."

"Do tell." Pease's tongue darted around his lips. "How you figure to manage it? Phil Royer's a kind of tough man to push around."

"As my boss knows." Dork Wallace had come up beside them. "He's been trying for ten years to run Royer off."

The rancher stabbed a finger at Wallace's face. "You keep out of this, Dork. This here lady needs help."

Wallace gave the girl a sardonic grin. "Help . . . You don't know what you'd let yourself in for if this old man poked his grabby fingers into your business."

Pease yelped. "Keep out, I said."

Wallace spoke to the girl again, casually. "The old coyote has been conniving for ten years to get hold of the Twin R for himself, and every move he made he was singed. Right now that think-box of his is figuring how he can use you and your claim to tuck that spread in his own pocket."

Pease swelled like a pouter pigeon and shrieked. That was the word Wallace had long ago decided best described the rancher's raging voice.

"Clear out of here, you bird brain . . ." He started to swear, then caught himself in the girl's presence. "Damn it, you're fired. For good. This time I mean it."

Wallace winked at Ann Royer. "See? Just like I said."

"Out . . . Out." The gun at Pease's hip looked too big for the small hand that clawed toward it with striking speed and bent it out of the holster.

He did not level it. Dork's hand was there, closing around the wrist, his long free fingers easily twisting the butt out of the ranchman's grip.

"You ought to be more careful, boss. You'll blow off a toe."

The little man was purple. The words spewing out of his mouth were culled from the gutter dregs of border barrooms, half English, half Spanish, woman listening or no.

Calmly, as if he had heard the performance many times before, and an impressive performance it was, Dork Wallace broke the gun, emptied the shells into his hand and then his pocket, and laid the useless weapon on the top pole of the corral fence. Without a word he turned and swung up to the saddle he had left only minutes before. He never looked back. He knew Ace Pease was shaking both clenched fists in the air after him. He followed the ranch lane three miles to where it ended at the main eastwest road. He turned into that, eastward for Del Rio rather than west toward Beldos Crossing.

This time, he told himself, he was through. He had taken a lot off the old rooster because the job paid so well. But there were limits past which no man should go.

He had no doubt that when the temper cooled Pease would want him back. It was a tough crew the old man ran and there were few foremen who could stay on top of them. Several times in the past he had had to fight some new hand to show the man he was boss. Not because Pease had made him foreman but because he was the better man.

It was beginning to grow dark. He rode another five miles, then turned aside into a clump of spiny, high brush, beat it with a stick for snakes, hobbled the horse, and spread his blanket. He did not trouble with eating but made up a batch of sour dough starter and flour to rise for morning, rolled a cigarette, and sat smoking until the fat stars were out, then lay down. He was asleep in three minutes.

Dork Wallace had learned a long time ago how to relax utterly. He had first ridden up the trail in '71, eleven years old at the time yet big enough to handle a man's chores. He did not remember the mother who had died in birthing him and his father had been a small-time gambler floating from one town to the next, always half drunk, always a loser when the chips were really down. Dork had no idea where the man was or even if he were still alive.

He had stumbled on and joined the cattle drive Ace Pease and two neighbors were putting together and he had worked for the Lazy P ever since.

At daybreak he roused, stiff from the ground, thinking vaguely that it was getting past the time when he had enjoyed a night in the bush. He built a small fire, boiled coffee, browned his biscuits and refried red beans, and made his meal. By six o'clock he was in the saddle again, pushing eastward.

The land had the warm smell of coming spring, the desert flowers made small bright patches after the recent rain, the creek was up with runoff, and a jay scolded as he passed its perch. He did not hurry.

It was four in the afternoon before he raised the distant silhouette of Del Rio. He rode the full length of the main street to reach Thorngood's livery, slapped the bay into the corral, and told the hostler to let him cool out, then water and grain him.

He left the saddle, blanket roll, and what remained of his tote bag in the barn office and walked back to the street, staying as much as possible under the wooden awnings that sheltered most of the slatted sidewalk until he reached the entrance of the Mermaid bar.

Dutch Kelly had chosen the name in honor of the garish, voluptuous painting he had brought with him and given prominent display above the long counter.

Inside it was hotter than it had been on the street. The lone bartender occupied the dragging time swatting at sluggish flies with a folded newspaper. He looked up as Wallace clicked through the swinging doors, waved the paper as a kind of salute, and brightened.

"Hello, stranger, long time no see. How's the Lazy P?"

"Normal when I left. Old man shrieking his skull out."

Austin Crabb grinned. Pease's tantrums were famous all along the valley. "Someday he'll blow the top off and splatter the ceiling with blood."

Wallace shook his head. "Can't. He ain't got no blood. I'll have a whiskey with a beer chaser."

Crabb set out a bottle, a small glass, and drew a stein of beer. It was Kelly's boast that the Mermaid was the only saloon in east Texas with an ice-making machine. Wallace swallowed the whiskey, then sipped appreciatively at the stein. By suppertime the room had filled. Three bartenders were on duty and Dutch Kelly presided over the poker game beginning in the rear.

Wallace left, continued the two blocks to the Statesman Hotel and turned in at the dark, narrow lobby.

Boyce Comstock, the owner, behind the desk, reached across to shake hands. "Going to be here long?"

"Can't tell. I've been fired or quit or both."

The hotelman chuckled. "Not again."

Wallace shrugged. "I mean to make this permanent. I've been screamed at by that fishwife long enough."

"Give you odds you'll be back on the Lazy P in a week." Comstock twisted the ledger and offered a pen.

Wallace signed the ink blotched page without taking the bet. Above his signature he read *Patricia Royer*, which meant Phil Royer's daughter must be in town. He saw her when he went into the dining room, eating at a back table with another woman. She did not look toward him. He had seen her several times but had never spoken to her.

He took an empty place at the big community table most of the hotel guests used and found himself across from Lee Dawson who edited the *Del Rio Sun*, and Spangler Cooper, a leading lawyer.

Both nodded to him. He could not claim to know either of them well but he rather liked the short, red-headed editor. For the lawyer he had no feeling either way, except that there was a cold and calculating manner that did not set well.

Their talk was about the cattle market, which was good, and Dork listened idly as the fat, perspiring waitress dealt steak, boiled potatoes, and cabbage before him. The cabbage was cooked gray-blue and Wallace did not touch it. The steak was tough, not properly hung, and the potatoes were a watery mush. The Statesman was not noted for its kitchen.

He ate the meat, left the rest, and went back to the lobby, biting off the end of a Cuban cigar bought earlier at the bar, lit it, anchored it between strong white teeth, and retreated to the porch. There, in a cane-backed chair with his feet on the rail, he watched the desultory traffic pass before him. Del Rio seldom changed and the habits of its people varied little.

The night marshal, Monk Hobart, came along the sidewalk trying doors. A cadaverous, mousy man, he looked about as effective as a lay preacher. But outlaws and drunk cowboys had discovered he could draw a gun with the best of them and could shoot out the pip on the ace of spades at a hundred yards. He saw Wallace, smiled a shy greeting, and moved deliberately on about his rounds, disappearing into the dark throat of Hop Alley on his way to his evening meal at Big Lizzy's house of pleasure.

The screen door behind Dork Wallace flapped open and he turned his head. For a full instant his dark eyes locked with those of Patricia Royer, an odd light gray. In the second before she looked away Wallace realized she knew who he was and beneath her level stare he saw a quick curiosity. The other woman was not with her. She crossed the gallery, descended the two steps, crossed the board sidewalk, and walked diagonally over the rutted street. She paused while two freight wagons passed, then moved on to knock on the Princess's door and go inside.

Wallace had never learned for certain who the Princess was or where she had come from. Rumor had it she was a gypsy, although she could be Mexican from below the river. She was short, given to fat, and at times sat stonily in a straight chair outside her house watching the Del Rio people go by. Indoors she told fortunes, using elaborate charts, cards with the zodiac emblems on them, and a crystal ball.

One night Wallace and three Lazy P riders had got drunk and paid two dollars apiece to have their futures read. It was his later opinion the two dollars would have been better invested with one of Big Lizzy's girls.

It piqued his curiosity that Pat Royer should visit over there. She had a level look about her steady eyes, a no-nonsense manner that had led him to believe she would be the last to be taken in by a charlatan such as the Princess.

He tossed away the butt of the cigar and rose, pressed to do something, anything to break the monotony of the evening. Of his life in fact. But what was there to do? Del Rio offered three amusements. You could drink at Dutch Kelly's or visit Big Liz, or play poker. He decided on poker although he was indifferent to gambling.

There was an empty chair at Kelly's table and he slid into it, nodding to the players around it. The game was California draw, open on anything, nothing wild. Dutch Kelly did not play. He dealt, took a cut of every pot for the house and let the players battle the hands out among themselves.

The game was small. Two raises and a fifty cent limit. Merchants or riders in off the range, Kelly's patrons were not rich. The action dragged. Dork Wallace bought a bottle to help his boredom. His mind was not on the cards. Maybe, he thought, he had been in this country too long. He might go someplace else, where things were doing. Dallas. Or Kansas City. Even San Francisco.

Two hours later and most of the whiskey gone he rose, pocketed two dollars and two bits in winnings, and with the heel of the bottle tucked in his arm for a nightcap at the hotel he stepped out into the night heat of the street and looked up the dim canyon of the roadway.

Light lay out from the Statesman's lobby window in a bright rectangle across the thick dust. Other than the saloon behind him, the hotel in front and Big Lizzy's on up beyond, Del Rio was dark. The town seemed asleep. Then a woman's voice, protesting, reached Wallace.

"Let me pass. Get out of my way."

Several male voices, laughing, obviously drunk, drowned her out. Dork Wallace hesitated. It could be one of Lizzy's girls, although they were not allowed to set foot on Main Street. Then he heard her again and a tremor in her words held his attention.

"Let me go, I said. My father will have you whipped."

Now Wallace knew who it was. He had seldom heard her speak but the voice was distinctive. It was Pat Royer and she was in trouble.

He moved quickly, jumping into the road so his boot heels would not hammer a hollow warning on the sidewalk. There were three of them, black shapes against the block of light from the hotel. He did not know who they were but the shape of the hats and the bulge of holsters should make them riders in from a ranch for a monthly drunk.

"Come on, sweetie, just a little kiss . . ."

One man's hand had her wrist. Wallace's eyes were becoming accustomed to the dark and he saw her fight back but the man was too strong. She gave a gasping cry as the rider pushed his unshaven face against hers and fought to find her lips.

Wallace took the last yards in a flying leap, caught the man's shoulder and spun him, breaking the grip on the girl. The man cursed, drunk and graphic, and his hand swept to his hip, but Dork already had the bottle raised and brought it down across the skull. The glass broke but even through the hat the blow was hard enough to drive the man down. The knees folded and he collapsed and lay still.

The other pair charged Wallace from opposite sides. His headway carried him past and they jarred into each other full force, hung together for a minute, then shoved against each other, and turned to charge again.

Dork Wallace had used the time to draw his gun and as they came at him from the same direction he slammed the barrel across the nearest man's face. The nose broke and the man fell away.

Then the last man was on Wallace, hooking a fist in his stomach that doubled him over and before he could straighten bringing up a bony knee against his ribs.

Dork Wallace sat down. Vaguely he saw the man above him swing his boot back and then forward, aiming at Wallace's head. He swayed aside, grabbed for the boot and caught it, jerked and upended the man, brought him down to crack his head on the edge of the sidewalk with a popping sound.

20

None of the three moved. Wallace climbed slowly and watchfully to his feet, leary that one or more might be playing possum, setting himself for another attack, but none came. Pat Royer had been knocked down as the rider threw her away from him to meet Wallace's charge. He was aware that she had rolled to her knees and scrambled against the building, out of the way of the fight, and he looked across at her.

"Thank you." Her words were clear and steady. "Are you hurt inside?"

Breathing sent sharp pain stabbing through his chest and Wallace thought a rib might be cracked but he shook his head and when he could use his voice said quietly, "The wind knocked out is all."

He bent to find the guns, easing the ache by the position. His lay on the sidewalk and the others were still holstered. He took them, tucked them into his belt and told the girl, "I'm going to the marshal's office with these. Will you come along or should I take you to the hotel first?"

"I'll come. I want to see him too."

They moved together down the street. Wallace wondered why Hobart had not already showed up with his usual instinct for being at a trouble spot almost before a flare occurred. They passed the bank and turned the corner. No light came from the office ahead, and that, too, was strange. Every time Dork had been in Del Rio overnight Monk Hobart had kept his lamps burning until dawn.

He pushed the door open and stood aside for Pat Royer, followed her in and went to the wall bracket, striking a match. As he touched the flame to the wick a series of grunting sounds made him spin. The spreading yellow glow showed him Monk Hobart sitting on the cot in the single cell fighting the gag tied in his mouth. His hands were fastened behind him and both ankles roped to the legs of the cot. The cell door stood wide open in mockery.

Wallace strode through and used his range knife to cut the wrists free first, then the ankles as Hobart yanked away the gag and sputtered half aloud curses, inhibited by the girl. Wallace did not ask for explanation. That would come or not in Hobart's own time, and it wasn't long.

"Those damn Rafferty brothers. I caught two of them stealing whiskey from Cap Myer's store and nailed them, then Clem slipped up behind me and put a gun in my back."

From outside the cell Patricia Royer said, "Then they got drunk and waylaid me on the street and I'd have been in a pickle if Dork Wallace hadn't knocked them out."

"All three at once?"

Hobart watched as Wallace took the guns out of his belt, walked to the desk and dropped them there and told the marshal, "I'll help you bring them in if you say so. I think they're still out cold."

"Show me." Hobart snatched up the big gun they had taken from him, slammed it into his holster and stumped to the door looking anything but ineffective.

The Raffertys were still sprawled on the sidewalk. Monk Hobart grunted his satisfaction, told Wallace to watch them and continued on to the alley that took him behind the Myer store, coming back with the two-wheeled cart Myer used for deliveries. He dropped the brace that kept it level and with Wallace slung the limp bodies on the deck. Pat Royer followed as they pushed the cart to the office and waited while they laid the Raffertys in a row on the cell floor. Monk locked the grille and hung the key on its nail, saying to Pat, "You want to charge them, honey?"

"I'd rather not, Monk." She gave him a half smile. "You've got enough to hold them on the robbery without my starting tongues wagging and putting Dad on the warpath."

"Guess you're right," Monk admitted. "And I don't think they'll remember when they wake up. Hope they don't." He looked toward Wallace. "They're nasty customers if they get it in for a body, son. Look out for yourself. And much obliged for the hand."

Wallace flipped a finger to dismiss any obligation the marshal might feel, touched the girl's arm, and said he would walk her to the hotel. On the street she volunteered a bit of information by way of further thanking Dork.

"Those brothers have been out to hurt my father ever since he found them with a fire and running iron and ran them off our range. Tonight they saw a chance to hit at him by picking on me. I don't know what would have happened if you hadn't interfered."

"Nothing very much." His tone was easy. "Men don't harass a good woman in this country."

"I can't class these as men . . . and I hope you weren't badly injured in the rescue."

He still had the catch in his chest that made a full breath painful but he smiled and shook his head. At the hotel he held the door for her and went in after her. Boyce Comstock also left a lamp burning low all night but his desk was empty. Wallace knew from past experience that a coffeepot would be on the back of the stove for reveling guests who came in late and he told the girl this.

"I'm going to have a cup. Would you like one to help you relax?"

"Sounds fine." He did not see the little smile. Pat Royer, raised on the ranch, did not let frights hang on after danger was gone, and it was a new experience to be treated as if she were fragile by this soft-spoken, laconic man.

They walked the length of the dark dining room and through to the scrubbed kitchen. Wallace took thick cups off the shelf, found cream in the cool room and sugar in the cabinet, and saw a bottle of Comstock's private whiskey there, and held it up.

"Want yours laced?"

She reached for the bottle and poured a good ounce in each cup. He added coffee, saying, "Not every woman will drink liquor except as a medicine . . . I guess this qualifies as that."

She laughed, a good sound. "Not every woman has Phil Royer for a father. I've been having whiskey royal with him since I was twelve when mother died."

24

They drank in silence. There was an easiness about being with this man. His quiet was not forced and she liked it that he did not press a conversation. The warm whiskey made some bond and she finally said, musing, "It's strange how you can think you know something about a person and then discover all your notions are wrong."

"How so?"

"I've been seeing you in town these last ten or twelve years, and always judged you by the outfit you ride for."

His lips came up in a wry twist. "Rode."

She chuckled. "Again? I've heard how that old man gets mad and fires you and then comes running after you over and over. You're very patient with him."

Dork's grin was faint. "Was patient. I guess maybe he fired me once too often."

"Really? Then what will you do?"

"Don't know yet, I just rode in this afternoon. Look around, maybe sign on with some trail herd heading north. I've been hankering to see what the Montana and Dakota hills look like."

"And leave Texas?" She sounded incredulous.

He laughed at her. "There speaks a true Texan. I didn't say I was leaving for good. But I'd like a look and a road leads both ways. I don't like it I can ride back . . . More coffee?"

She set down the empty cup and stood up. "I'd better get some sleep. Dad is due in from Eagle Pass on the stage tomorrow and I don't want circles under my eyes to meet him with. Again, my thanks, and good night."

He rose and watched her go, then poured himself more coffee and more whiskey. It amused him to think of Comstock's explosion when he discovered the level in his private bottle lowered, but he would leave the bar price of the drinks on the shelf. He sat down again, lit a cigar, and sipped, daydreaming, building fantasies of what might lie ahead up trails he had never ridden.

CHAPTER
THREE

Old man Pease was a familiar sight in Del Rio. Owner of the largest ranch along the valley, he used the town more or less as unofficial headquarters. He came driving the buckboard behind a span of beautifully matched duns. That was his extravagance, horses. He skimped on everything else but he would not have a scrub horse on the ranch.

Ann Royer rode the hard seat at his side and three riders trailed them up Main Street to the center of the business district. Pease liked to brag that in his long scramble to his present eminence he had made more enemies than anyone else in Texas and it was his practice not to venture into any town without a few of his hands as escort.

He reined in, dropped to the dusty road, and raised a gallant hand to help the girl down, then beckoned a rider up to take the rig on to the livery, and while the man dismounted Pease raked the street with fierce eyes. It was the habit of the rancher, nourished by his distrust of everyone, to look for danger everywhere. Seeing nothing to disturb him he clamped a small claw around the girl's upper arm and steered her across the sidewalk to the stairs that led to the combined residence and office of the lawyer Spangler Cooper.

Dork Wallace had not yet ridden out. The Rafferty brothers were still in jail but until Phil Royer arrived on the stage and took his daughter away from the town Dork would stick around. There was no real reason why he should concern himself about her, but he had stepped in once and somehow that made her safety his business until her father took over again.

Screened in the semidark hotel lobby, Wallace watched the arrival of Ace Pease with the girl from Mexico. When he saw the bantam rancher start her up the steps against the side of Pfister's feed store his mouth made a silent O. The story was plain to read in the few minutes since they had come into sight. Pease was making medicine. Meddling in the girl's affair, and certainly not intending to help her. Part of the reason would be to further annoy Phil Royer for the pure devilment of it. But in the main Pease would be sniffing for ways by which he could come into possession of at least some of Twin R's holdings. A creeping encroachment on other properties had succeeded through the years in expanding the Lazy P in other directions, but Royer had held his line intact at the bank of Wolf's Run until now. Wallace wondered how much longer the stream boundary would hold Pease back.

On the second floor across the street Spangler Cooper was about to hear the first overture toward crossing over. He had been at his window when the buckboard rolled in and stopped, and he knew he would be visited and went to make ready. When his door opened he was at his roll-top desk flanked on one side by a letterpress and on the other by a single shelf of law books. A tall man with Indian-straight black hair and a hook nose between bright, piercing eyes, he waited.

Cooper had become Pease's lawyer six years earlier, a month after he had appeared in Del Rio leading a pack animal that carried the letterpress and books. He thought he knew his client well but Pease had a habit of pulling surprises like rabbits out of a hat, and those challenges spiced an otherwise mostly bland and boring practice.

When the girl was ushered in he rose hastily and bowed and said across her head, "Good to see you, sir." He still used the slow drawl of his native Carolina and unfailing courtesy, but the voice somehow rang a little false to trained ears, the manner bordered on the unctious. "Am I honored with a social call or y'all come in on business?"

It was a standard ceremony. Pease had never yet wasted a minute here in idle conversation. Cooper did not expect it and was not disappointed this time. Pease said immediately, "This here's little Annie Royer, Phil's niece, and the mangy coyote's done her wrong. Dead wrong. Spangler, you know he's a cur but it plumb takes my breath that he'd be low enough to beat a poor orphan girl out of her due inheritance. We got to help her get it back."

Left alone Pease could take an hour rambling around a subject before Cooper could make out what point he was aiming at, and to forestall that the lawyer straightened from touching his lips to the girl's hand and told the rancher, "Then you'd best let her tell me herself about her problem, so I see the picture clearly. Miss Royer, what is this inheritance?"

Pease always liked the center of the stage but in this case he thought the girl would create the impression he wanted on the lawyer so he stayed quiet while she again recited all she had lost of family and ranches.

She finished with a little lift of hope. "It was an accident that I rode into the Lazy P, or maybe the angels guided me to someone who offered to help get justice from my uncle. Can you . . . ?"

Without looking away from her Cooper said, "And what is Pease going to get out of it?"

"Get?" The girl looked startled.

Pease interrupted before Cooper could go on, sputtering with indignation. "Can't a man do a little for a friendless, defenseless orphan out of the charity in his heart and not expect to be paid? Hell of a note."

Better than anyone Spangler Cooper knew the depth of the rancher's selflessness, but it would not be good business for him to warn the girl and he said only, "Very well. What do you expect me to do?"

"Get her ranch for her of course. What did you think?" Pease still blustered.

"How?"

"You're the lawyer. You tell us."

"I'll look into it. But first, Miss Royer, are you sure your father did not deed the ranch to his brother?"

"Very sure. He only gave him the power of attorney."

"You yourself, have you ever signed anything like a quitclaim for instance?"

"Indeed not."

Pease asked suspiciously, "A power of attorney signed by a dead man isn't binding on his heirs, is it?"

"I don't think so," Cooper said. "I'll have to look that up. I've never been in an involvement like this before."

"Do that for starters," Pease ordered, "and let us know. We'll be at the hotel until you find out."

Cooper bowed them out, then sat down and rested his chin on the steeple of his fingers, humming to himself while he projected how much of the Twin R spread his client would reach for first and how much profit he could make for himself out of a law case.

Dork Wallace had moved out to a chair on the hotel gallery to see Ann Royer's reaction when she came from the lion's den of Cooper's office. He wondered if he could tell from her expression how much she had learned about Frank Ace Pease in that interview. But when they came down the stairs she still looked trusting. It was too bad, but he had said as much as he could to warn her in the Lazy P yard the day before and plainly she had not heeded. They crossed toward him and were at the foot of the gallery steps before Pease looked up and discovered Wallace above him. Then Pease roared at him.

"What the hell you doing here? You're supposed to be at the ranch starting the roundup and you know it."

Wallace said evenly, "You fired me."

"Come off it," Pease grunted. "You got me riled and you know I didn't mean it."

"This time I'll stay fired, Ace."

Pease swelled and reddened and his voice went up. "You can't do that, Dork."

"Why not? I . . ."

"Who's going to run the place? Who'd keep the hands in line?" He made an effort to hold onto the rising temper and put out a pleading hand. "Dork . . . That chestnut you're always looking at. He's all yours right now."

"Sorry."

That Dork would neither give in nor even argue, even bargain, sent the voice shrieking up the scale and drew hidden laughter from people on the street while some ducked into doorways to watch. With both fists shaking above his head Pease threatened.

"You leave me, I'll run you clean out of the country. I ain't going to sit by quiet and see you go to work for somebody else in this valley. I'll run you so far . . ."

Wallace turned his attention to Ann Royer and said quietly, "You offered me a job yesterday, ma'am. Is it still open?"

Before she could speak Pease broke in, snarling, "You hire him and you can kill your own snakes. I ain't laying out no money to fight Phil Royer if you take on this no-good bonehead hound and that's fact. You hear?"

Wallace had expected that, had only asked her to give her an example of the rancher's vengefulness, but she still did not see danger. She knuckled under, telling him, "I guess that tells the story, doesn't it?"

She went on alone into the hotel and Wallace said evenly, "Ace, I'll bet you took the pennies off your dead mother's eyelids. You ought to be ashamed of yourself."

"For what?" Abruptly the rage was gone and Pease was hurt. "All I aim to do is get that girl's ranch for her and run it for her. You going to fault me for that?"

"For gradually taking it away from her I will."

"You don't think I'd . . ."

Pease stopped in mid-sentence because Patricia Royer came out through the door. He turned his back and tramped down the sidewalk toward the Mermaid bar, bristling. Pat watched after him, then smiled at Wallace.

"Are you still fired or did he come for you again?"

"Still fired. I'm not the reason he's in town."

"What then, at such a busy time?"

"He's getting ready to grab your ranch."

"Oh? How this time?"

Instead of a direct answer Wallace said, "Did you see a girl in the lobby a couple of minutes ago?"

"One went through as I was coming out. Who is she?"

"You didn't recognize her?"

"No. Should I?"

"The name Ann Royer mean anything to you?"

"My cousin? Is that her? I've never seen her." She began to turn toward the door. "I'll go introduce myself."

"Better not, yet. She claims her father owned Twin R and she inherits it."

For a long moment Pat Royer stared alternately at the door and at Wallace without speaking, then she crossed and sank into the chair at Wallace's side.

"I don't understand what you're saying, Dork."

He watched her face and told her, "She says at the end of the war her father went to Mexico, gave Phil a power of attorney to sell the ranch for him but that Phil kept hold of it for himself. Do you know anything about that story?"

She was unguardedly shocked, shaking her head with increasing vigor and then bursting out, "Indeed I do not. That is absurd. My father owns that ranch . . . everybody in the country knows it."

"Believes it, anyway. Well, you can ask him in a minute. Here comes the stage now."

The coach had just dropped over the shelf of the rise and the driver brought the six-horse team down and into the main street pounding, full out. The office was next door to the hotel and the rig wheeled up there, throwing dust and drawing idlers. The door opened and two women came down the step. Phil Royer was next to the ground.

Royer was big, four inches over six feet, with powerful shoulders and legs and a waist as slender as it had been twenty years before. He waited at the boot while the driver passed out luggage, then with his grip swinging loosely against his leg turned toward the hotel, saw his daughter, and waved. Then he stopped with one foot lifted, seeing Dork Wallace in the chair beside the girl. His face darkened and he went on with angry purpose. The girl rose to greet him and Royer took her arm, ignoring Wallace, half pushing her toward the door.

"Come inside, Pat."

She held back against his tugging, saying sharply, "Wait, Dad. Dork Wallace has something to tell you."

Without a glance toward the seated man Royer told his daughter, "He has nothing to say that I want to hear. Come."

She jerked away and held her ground, her eyes angry and her voice tart. "You had just better listen to him whether or not you want to. For your information, last night Dork risked his life to help me. The Rafferty boys were drunk and stopped me on the street and started mauling me. Dork jumped them, all three, and knocked the daylights out of them . . ."

Phil Royer showed quick concern for the girl and the mouth under his groomed mustache widened to a thin line.

"Where are the Raffertys now?"

"In jail, where Monk and Dork hauled them in Myer's cart."

Finally Royer looked full at Wallace and said flatly, "I thank you." His expression would have been the same if he had bitten into a green quince. It hurt him to admit that he owed anything to a man who rode for Frank Pease. He tried once again to take his daughter off the porch but she still pulled away.

"There's more you have to hear, Dad. There's a girl in there who says she is your niece and that our ranch belongs to her, not to us."

Phil Royer started a gesture of impatience, then stopped it and sounded curious. "Did she tell you this?"

"I haven't spoken to her. She told Dork and he warned me."

Royer rounded on Wallace again, his words clubbing. "What is this, another of Frank Pease's little nightmares you're pitching?"

Wallace's smile was mildly mocking. He knew Royer looked down on him and it had never mattered to him and did not now.

"It wasn't to begin with and I'm not pitching it. Ann Royer told me the story before she knew there was a Frank Pease. But he brought her to town today and they went up to see Spang Cooper."

Phil Royer looked at the upstairs window across the street, his face changing, turning troubled, and the girl, seeing this, said in a worried tone, "It isn't true, Dad, is it? Doesn't the ranch belong to us?"

He took too long to answer, but when the words came they were definite enough.

"It does, certainly."

She sighed in quick relief. "Then she's lying?"

"It isn't that simple, Pat. It's my fault, I suppose, but it never occurred to me there would be any question."

The relief vanished as quickly as it had come and she looked bewildered, saying, "I don't understand. What is it?"

Phil Royer brought his attention away from the window, around to his daughter, and then to Wallace, brooding on the rider, still hostile, obviously not

36

wanting to make any explanation with Dork listening, then changed his mind.

"Best to bring it out in the open I guess. Patricia, at the end of the war my brother Howard swore he would never live in the United States again. We had already been driven out of Carolina to Texas and he was bitter. I tried to talk him out of leaving because there was revolution in Mexico but he wouldn't listen to me. There was no possibility of selling a Texas ranch then, the whole state was broke. The only people with money were the carpetbaggers, Northerners, a horde of locusts, so he gave me Twin R for my help in rounding up a herd of cattle gone wild during the war and driving them below the line.

"Because the courthouses were controlled by the carpet-baggers he did not give me a deed. The tax office would have demanded a transfer tax that we couldn't possibly have raised. To get around that he gave me his power of attorney. I suppose I should have gotten a deed long ago but it didn't seem necessary. Now, I assume he's dead?"

"That's what the girl told me. Her father and mother were murdered by raiders."

Pain contorted the rancher's face and his daughter pressed her fingers against her mouth, watching him in sympathy, then he drew a deep breath and put the loss behind him, something that could not be undone and must be borne but not dwelt on. He looked down to Wallace again.

"How did my niece meet Pease?"

"Accident. She came riding across the river a couple of days ago looking for Twin R and I met her on the trail."

"You took her to him?"

"Wrong guess. She got there on her own. I warned her about him. He blew up and fired me and this time I won't go back."

Royer looked skeptical, shrugged, and asked, "What are you doing then?"

"Resting." Dork Wallace lifted his boots to the rail, his mouth twisting. "I want to sit here and see what happens when Spang Cooper and the old man figure out how to take your ranch away from you."

CHAPTER
FOUR

Tom Foster was alone at the line-camp. Usually he had three or four men riding fence but the roundup had started and he had sent all of the spare crew with the wagon to join the other four ranches working slowly across the Burnt Range just north of Phil Royer's holdings.

He stepped out of the cabin into the cool morning air, walked to the creek that wandered through the thick carpet of meadow grass, and washed his face and hands in the quiet water.

Sounds of harness made him straighten and he saw a group of riders top out of a swale and run their animals toward him. Something in the manner of their coming startled him. He hesitated briefly, then began running toward the cabin door. He did not reach it. The leading rider had shaken out a loop and the noose fell around Foster's shoulders, jerked taut, and yanked him off his feet. He sprawled on his side hard.

It might be sport but he was furious. He struggled up and glared at the mounted men surrounding him, recognizing them as some of Frank Pease's hands although he had never had anything to do with them. He sputtered, spitting sand and grass, trying to work the rope off but the man holding it whipped it tight again and there were no smiles on the hard faces.

"Stand quiet, you," the man with the rope warned. "Joe, go on to the cabin and fetch out Foster's gear. Chuck, you saddle his horse."

"Just hold on here," Foster raged. "What the hell you think you're trying?"

"Not trying. We're taking over Twin R."

Tom Foster's mouth fell open, gaping. "Taking over? You gone crazy?"

"Don't think so." The man dallied the rope expertly, flipped the noose up over Foster's head and coiled it. "Here's a piece of advice. If you want to keep that skin you're wearing whole, you'll climb your horse and ride out of here. We got orders to hang you if we find you in this country again."

Outrage held Foster speechless. Who did these saddle bums think they were? He was on his employer's land. He was foreman for Phil Royer. He fought for his voice and finally managed, "If I had a gun . . ."

"But you don't. If you had you'd be dead now. Count yourself lucky."

The rider called Joe came carrying Foster's war bag and blanket at the same time Chuck led the saddled pinto from the corral. The leader hung his rope on the horn and unholstered his forty-five.

"Mount up, and don't go to the ranch house. You'd run into a peck of trouble there."

Wordless and shaking with anger Foster stepped to his saddle and rode out, knowing they would watch him

40

out of sight, and he did not head for the ranch but north toward the roundup crews.

There was indeed trouble at the Twin R headquarters. Frank Pease with Ann Royer and twelve riders had quietly moved in during the night. All of Royer's men were away at the roundup, no one on the place except Royer and his daughter. There was not even a cook in the cookshack.

It was still dark when Phil Royer came into his kitchen, found the lamps burning, the stove hot, a strange girl, Frank Pease, and a dozen hands around his table eating breakfast. He stopped in the doorway, cold with anger.

"What are you all doing here?"

Ann put down her coffee cup. "I asked them to come with me."

Royer looked at her, stone faced. "And by what right do you ask anyone to come into my house, eat my food, and make themselves at home?"

She told him calmly, "It isn't your house, Uncle Phil. It is mine."

He stared in disbelief. The room was silent. Then Patricia Royer slipped past her father. She showed no surprise at the invasion. Her father had brushed aside Dork Wallace's warning as an incredibility and shrugged off her urging that he talk to a lawyer to learn where they stood. So this was the result and it looked to her as if it were too late. She walked down the table to the stove, poured two cups of coffee, took one back to her father, then turned and examined the other girl with a long study.

Under the steady gaze the girl from Mexico got flustered and snapped. "What are you staring at?"

Pat said quietly, "I want to see what a highway robber actually looks like, Cousin Ann."

Frank Pease and his men chuckled, then Pease wiped his face empty of laughter and stabbed a fork toward Royer.

"You've got one half hour to load up your personal gear and clear out. You can take the buckboard but leave it at the livery for us to pick up."

Phil Royer looked down on the little rancher with full contempt. "You miserable little runt, I am not going one foot out of this house."

Frank Pease's temper started toward the boiling point. He lifted a shaking fist but the girl beside him laid her hand on it, smiled, whispered something, and he choked down his voice to a snarl.

"How you think you're going to keep from it? I'll tell you once more is all. You're leaving one way or another, your choice. Go on your own or my boys take you out at the end of a rope. Which will it be?"

Pat put a hand under her father's arm, saying, "Come, Dad, let's get packed," and turned him out of the kitchen.

Half an hour later they drove out of the lane, Pat handling the team and Phil frozen rigid at her side facing square ahead, aloof, ignoring the crowd that watched them. It was well after noon when they drew into Del Rio's Main Street and the girl stopped before the hotel. Royer appeared to wake from a dream, climbing slowly to the sidewalk and going for the porter to help with the baggage, then telling him to take the buckboard on to the livery. He helped his daughter down, ushered her into the lobby and to the desk where Boyce Comstock was going over his monthly books, saying in a chill, faraway voice, "Our usual rooms, Boyce."

The hotel man squirmed and flushed unhappily. "Well, Phil . . . I don't know . . . I guess I'll have to ask you to pay in advance . . ."

Royer had already picked up the pen to register. He stopped with it poised. "You what?"

"I'm right sorry . . . but . . ."

He looked sorry. He looked as if he wished the floor would swallow him. Royer turned his back and said to his daughter in a hollow voice, "Wait here, Pat, while I go to the bank."

He walked with a military stiffness out of the lobby, stretched to full height, his wide shoulders square, under tight control, his face lead colored under the heavy tan, and cater-cornered the street to the bank. He wrote a check for a hundred dollars and presented it silently at the cashier's window. Behind the wicket Paul Gilmore ran a forefinger around inside his celluloid collar, picked up the paper by one corner and stepped out of Royer's long reach, saying huskily, "I'll have to ask about this . . ."

Royer watched him scuttle to the president's office, then Hyde Stewart came to the door also holding the check as if it burned his fingers, beckoned and said, "Phil . . . Step in here a minute."

Royer crossed to the door and went through, towering over the round man he faced. "What the hell is going on around here, Stewart?"

The banker put his desk between them before he said, "That's what I want to ask you. Spangler Cooper was in here first thing this morning. Put an attachment on your account."

"How can he do that?"

"Why, you didn't carry it in your name. It's carried as the Twin R account."

"That's right."

"So he got a court order. He claims you do not hold legal title to the ranch, that your niece inherited it. Is that so, Phil?"

Phil Royer sat down heavily without answering. He had the feeling of living a nightmare or trying to walk in quicksand. Yesterday he had been one of the most powerful men in that part of Texas. Now even the hotelkeeper who had known him for years would not trust him for a night's lodging. He had no cash. He never carried money. For years there had been no reason to. His credit had been unquestioned. Now, driven from his home, his bank account attached, his mind was frozen, and he did not know where to turn.

Hyde Stewart read the signs in the ashen face and the way Royer sat, a ramrod up his back, big hands clutched around his knees as though he waited for a death blow. He coughed to bring the rancher's attention back to the office and said softly, "Phil, there's a little in Pat's primping account as she calls it. That's in her name . . ."

Royer looked blank for a moment, then nodded, stood up stiffly, and stalked out. Pat, waiting at the hotel window, knew by the way he came there was more trouble. She met him at the door.

"What is it now, Dad?"

His voice was dry and toneless. "They've attached the ranch account. How much have you in yours?"

"Oh my dear . . . How wicked . . . I've maybe a hundred dollars, I'm not sure exactly."

"Sign a blank check for me. That can keep us from starving until I get my bearings, find out what to do."

She opened the small case stacked with their bags, took out the checkbook and signed a check. Royer hurried back to the bank before some other legal trickery could snatch that from him. Stewart looked up the girl's balance and gave him ninety-three dollars in small bills and said, "Now, will you please sit down and tell me what is going on at Twin R?"

Royer sat and told him bitterly. "My brother's daughter . . . I never saw her before this morning . . . believes he left the ranch to her and that I tried to steal it from her."

"I see. Can't you explain to her that he gave it to you and why you have no deed?"

"I can't explain anything, Hyde. Frank Pease and Spang Cooper got hold of her. They're backing her claim and you know as well as I do that if the court upholds her they'll find a way to take it away from her."

"I'll bet on that." The banker rocked back in his swivel chair, his eyes on the ceiling, narrow in thought. "Your brother is dead then?"

"That's what she says and the only way I could learn for sure would be to go to Mexico."

"She isn't married, is she?"

"I wouldn't think so since she's using the Royer name. Why?"

"You're not native Texan I know, but are you familiar with our law?"

"I'm no lawyer but I guess I know something about it. What are you getting at?"

The banker had a soft face and a baby smile that began to play around his mouth as he looked down and into Royer's tight face.

"You do know our basic law is borrowed from the Spanish, not the English common law of most of the rest of the country?"

"I've heard so." Royer sounded impatient, wondering where the rambling discourse was leading.

Stewart's smile widened. "Under Spanish law a woman cannot control her own property, Phil."

Royer's jaw dropped. "I wasn't aware . . ."

"Thought maybe not. If a woman is married her husband controls whatever she owns. If she is single her nearest male relative has the control. As her uncle, aren't you her nearest male relative?"

"Oh?" Royer said it slowly, unsure. "Are you certain of that, Hyde?"

"I ought to be. This bank has acted as trustee for a good many widows and orphans and we've had some thorny hassles trying to protect them from unscrupulous relatives." He frowned. "I wonder how Spang Cooper thinks he could get around that."

46

The dazed bewilderment washed out of Phil Royer and the mire of helplessness changed to solid ground under his feet. In the moment his vitality was back, his mind functioning again. He whistled a low note, then grinned.

"Hyde, I think I can have a little fun out of this after all. I'll take care of Howard's child, not pack her off alone, but oh am I going to enjoy watching Frank Pease pull in his horns. First, though, I have to put together a new crew tough enough to throw Pease off the ranch before they steal every cow on it."

Stewart nodded, saying, "You could do worse than start with Dork Wallace. He handled Pease's hardcases a long time."

Phil Royer had a scornful laugh and a slash of his hand through the air. "Wallace. When old man Pease whistles Dork will trot back wagging his tail like a dog. He's done it again and again."

Stewart raised his brows and pursed his mouth. "Don't believe so this time. He was in to see me last evening asking if I knew of a job. He said he'd intended riding north but had decided to stay and watch the show and wanted to be in town. I didn't know what show he meant then but I guess now he meant this one . . . Up to you of course."

Royer disliked the idea. Wallace had been associated in his mind with Frank Pease's reputation a long time, but in fairness Stewart was right. The Lazy P foreman could handle men and better than anyone he knew the old man's quirks of thinking. He made his decision without more hesitation.

"Where is he?"

"Staying at Comstock's I think. Just now he's probably sitting in a poker game at Dutch Kelly's place."

Phil Royer stood up, a fresh brittle shine in his eyes, nodded at the banker, and left the office. He crossed briskly to the hotel, tossed twenty dollars on the worn counter and said flatly, "Take the baggage up, Boyce."

Comstock looked up from the money with a hangdog guilt, cleared his throat and ran the red tip of his tongue around his lips.

"Phil . . . I understood . . ."

"From Spang Cooper . . ."

The hotel man's face reddened and he said defensively, "Man has to protect himself, don't he?"

Royer turned his back and walked to Pat, sitting in a lobby chair. "Would you rather visit with Mrs. Ellis or wait in your room? I'll be a while."

The change in him was remarkable but with Comstock straining to hear what they said the girl asked no questions, only gave him an encouraging smile, and told her father she would stay in the room. With his back to the hotel man Royer closed one eye without moving another muscle of his face, a wink of assurance, and went out, striding to the Mermaid bar.

The evening crowd had not yet gathered. Dork Wallace and four other players at a rear table were the only men there. Wallace's hat brim was pulled down to shield his eyes from the overhead lamp. A half-filled whiskey bottle sat at his elbow and a cigar between his lips gave off a straight, vertical plume of blue smoke.

He had a stack of money before him and was apparently winning. Etiquette demanded that the hand should not be interrupted and Royer stood back until Wallace looked at his last card, palmed the five, fanned them, then tossed them on the table, then he stepped to the man's shoulder.

"See you a minute, Dork?"

Wallace brought his eyes up and showed faint surprise at seeing Royer. He hesitated a moment, then gathered his money with a sweep of a hand, and stuffed it carelessly into a pocket as he rose. He picked up the bottle by its neck and saying nothing went to a table at the far side of the room, waving with the bottle at the bartender for glasses. He dropped into a chair and Royer gingerly took the seat opposite. Neither spoke until the glasses arrived and Wallace poured both full. Wallace emptied his in a single swallow and set the glass on the table, watching Royer sip his.

"What's on your mind?"

Royer took his glass away from his lips. "Hyde Stewart tells me you're looking for a job. Would you work for me?"

Wallace emptied his face of the astonishment he felt and smiled faintly. "I'll work for the devil if he'll pay me enough. Come to think of it, I've worked for him a number of years."

"Make a difference that you'd be fighting Frank Pease?"

The gray eyes turned lively. "Fine with me."

"What was Ace paying you?"

"A hundred and found."

"I'll make it one fifty."

Wallace sank back in the chair, a corner of his mouth twisting up. "For that you want me to kill the old bastard?"

Royer matched the smile and felt an odd warming toward this man he had despised. "That could be the simple way and God knows I'm in the mood to say yes, but that isn't the job I have in mind. I want him and his riders run off my place."

Wallace stopped in the middle of filling the glasses again and this time his surprise was plain on his face. "You mean they're already out there?"

Phil Royer let the depth of his bitterness show. "They moved in before daylight. When I got up they were there, Pease, my niece, and twelve riders, sitting in my kitchen, breakfasting on my stores."

Dork had a way of laughing silently when he was particularly amused and his chest and shoulders shook now with the convulsions.

"Trust the old man to do things different. By the way, I have to say your niece is a handsome filly, whatever else she may be."

"Part of which I judge is, she's as mean as they come. At least her lawyer has done everything he can to hamstring me, even attached my back account. If Pat hadn't had a few dollars we'd be up the creek."

Wallace sobered and watched the rancher narrowly. "How did they manage that?"

"The account is in the Twin R name rather than my own. Spang Cooper claims it belongs to the ranch."

"Very neat. They do seem to have you trussed up. So what do you accomplish by running Pease off if you don't own the place?"

It was Phil Royer's turn to smile and his words had a roll of genuine pleasure to them. "So you're not native Texan either. Hyde Stewart tells me they've a law here that no woman in Texas can control her property. It rests with her nearest male relative."

Dork Wallace met the rancher's eyes and showed his appreciation of the overturning situation and lifted his glass in a toast.

"And I assume you qualify in the case of your niece?"

"I do."

"That I like. Very much. It would please me a lot to watch Ace Pease's face when he's reminded of that fact. He never was married so maybe he never heard about it, but I'm surprised at Spang Cooper for not taking it into consideration."

"So was I." The rancher frowned in puzzlement. "Maybe though he thought I wouldn't be aware of the law and he could bluff me . . . You'll take the job?"

"Provided I have a free hand to run the show."

"Meaning?"

"It will be a nasty fight, Royer, and I never thought your crew was very warlike."

"You're right on that," the rancher agreed. "Most of them have been with me for years and we've never had much trouble."

"So I'll have to put on some fighting men, people you wouldn't ordinarily want around."

Royer took a while, looking over the long room almost as if for escape from a necessity that stuck in his craw. His Twin R had been a place of serenity, of friendliness between himself and his crew and he had no liking for the kind of men Wallace meant. Then he sighed and nodded.

"Do what you have to, Dork."

"Next thing is money. Those I sign on will want to see some in advance. With your account frozen how are you going to pay them?"

Royer thought about that and finally said, "I think Stewart would give me a loan against the ranch since I'll be taking it back. How much do you need?"

"Pease regularly carries fifteen to twenty riders on his payroll, not all gun hands but just now ten of them can stand up to most arguments. I'll need to match them. You keep your regular crew for the ranch work. How many are there?"

"My foreman, Tom Foster, and seven riders. They're out on the roundup now."

"Good. Send word for them to keep away from the ranch after we see Hyde Stewart and make sure of the loan."

CHAPTER
FIVE

Bucko Sollars stood six foot seven without his boots and walked sideways through most doors. His voice could shake bottles on a backbar and he wore a thick black beard and shoulder length lank hair. The story was that in the past he had been lynched but survived and the hair hid the rope burns that still scarred his big throat.

Dork Wallace had never met the man but he knew that Sollars more than anyone else dominated the toughs of the country around Eagle Pass and that his name was feared as far away as Dallas and El Paso. He came off the afternoon stage and stood in the dust surveying the sprawling county seat.

Very little moved on the hot street. A few loafers squatted under the wooden awning using the coach's arrival as the day's excitement, eying Wallace speculatively as he walked past them into the stage office. The agent was handing the driver the mail pouch and Dork waited while he made notations of the several express items the coach had brought. Then as the driver went out he stepped to the counter.

"Do you know Bucko Sollars? Where I'd find him?"

The agent's eyes went over Wallace in the manner of saying anyone wanting Sollars was as welcome in town as the pox and he was careful of his voice that it should not offend the tall, rangy stranger.

"Probably in Billy Richard's saloon. Just past the hotel."

"Thanks," Wallace said, took time to light a cigar, then left the office, walked to the saloon and paused again inside the batwing doors to let his eyes accustom to the dim light after the bright sun of the street.

Sollars could never be mistaken for anyone else. He was alone at a table with a bottle of whiskey talking livestock prices with a man three tables away and his roaring voice overrode all other sound in the long room. Dork Wallace crossed to him and dropped unasked into a chair opposite the giant. Sollars glared at him, pushing the bearded chin forward.

"Who the hell are you?"

Dork's faint smile was easy. "Man here to offer you some good money."

For a moment the glare lingered while Sollars made up his mind whether to get mad at the interruption, then he threw his head back and brayed a laugh that filled the far corners.

"Just like Santy Claus, huh? Friend, you are just the man I need. The bums cleaned me out last night. Charley . . . bring the man a glass."

The bartender came and set a glass in front of Dork and Sollars stretched a log of an arm across to fill it and then his own. That emptied the bottle and the giant dropped it on the sawdust.

"Now. You got a name?"

"Dork Wallace."

"Never heard of you."

Dork lounged against the chair back, still smiling. "We're not all as well known as Bucko Sollars."

The man's shoulders swaggered and he tossed his drink down. "What's the story?"

"I've just been hired as foreman of Twin R ranch and I'm looking for a crew."

The big man snorted. "I don't punch cows, mister."

Dork said evenly, "That wasn't what I had in mind. Old Frank Pease has run Phil Royer off his ranch and the job is to boot Pease out."

"Well now" — the bold black eyes above the beard brightened — "how much would this little operation pay?"

Wallace took five hundred dollars in crisp new bills from his pocket and fanned them like cards on the table. "One hundred a month and found apiece. For you and nine more men. Can you recruit them?"

The man snapped his fingers up past his shoulder. "In five minutes."

"The five hundred is your advance."

They measured each other for their potential strength. Wallace did not trust Sollars who was capable of pocketing the money and reneging on the deal. Still, Sollars had a reputation to maintain and with men in the room watching he would lose standing if he did that. Sollars grinned at him and reached but Wallace's hand was quicker, scooping the bills into a deck and holding them.

"When you have nine men lined up."

Again Sollars debated getting mad but shrugged instead, shoved his chair back and rose, dwarfing everything around him. "Your horse outside?"

"I came over by stage."

"Go rent one at the livery and meet me back here in fifteen minutes."

Sollars tramped out with a rolling, heavy gait and ducked through the door, letting the bats swing back against Wallace's hands. He jerked a thumb toward the right to indicate where the livery was and himself turned left. Fifteen minutes later Dork was mounted and waiting in front of the saloon and a moment afterward Sollars rode around the corner on a slash-faced roan big enough to pull a stage. He beckoned and when Dork swung in beside him turned north up the street. Beyond the town in the near distance rose a range of hills or low mountains and Sollars flapped a hand toward them.

"Boys we're going to see don't like questions."

Wallace said evenly, "The only one I have is whether they'll take orders."

"From me they will."

"And from me. I won't have a man riding for me who won't."

Their eyes locked and held. Sollars' were the first to look away and they rode saying nothing more. At the bed of a dry creek Sollars swung up its course and a mile beyond they topped over a shoulder. Below it in a hollow a log house squatted. Sollars pulled up on the crest and sent his bull voice battering ahead.

"Hey, Luke . . ."

A man came into the door frame carrying a rifle, holding it ready while they rode down the grade, his attention on the man with Sollars, wary even when the giant eased himself in the saddle and told him, "This here's Dork Wallace, Luke. He's got a chore for me and nine boys."

Still watching Wallace the man spat from the corner of his mouth. "What's it pay?"

"Hundred and found."

Wallace added, "And furnish your own horse."

Luke lowered the gun then and glanced at Sollars for the first time. "Seems fair. Shall I round them up?"

"Yup. And meet me in town tomorrow ready to ride."

"How long we be gone?"

Sollars turned his head toward Wallace and Dork answered, "Could be several months. It's a fighting crew we'll go against."

Luke showed snaggle teeth in a wolfish grin, backed into the house, and closed the door. Sollars and Wallace headed back toward town with no more to say and reached it in time for Dork to catch the evening stage. The run south would be cooler than the trip up had been and Dork welcomed that.

He was satisfied with the day. The men who had worked under him for Pease might be hardcases but not one of them but would think twice about a fight with Bucko Sollars.

He told Phil Royer this next morning when he visited the rancher's hotel room. As he finished Patricia Royer said from her seat beside the window, "You mean to start a range war, don't you?"

Her father showed annoyance, started to say something, but Wallace beat him to it.

"That's just what I am trying to avoid. Nobody in his right mind wants to pull a gun against men like Sollars' crowd. It's a form of suicide. I'm banking on some of Ace Pease's hands quietly slipping over the hill when they hear who we're using."

The girl said unhappily, "But others won't and there will be killing. Couldn't we rely on a court order to make Pease give up?"

"Who," Wallace said, "would enforce it? One sheriff? Frank Pease is not going to move off that land unless a gun is held to his head. And that gun is Sollars."

"I suppose you're right, Dork, but it doesn't seem a decent thing to do . . ."

Her father said in sudden savagery, "Life isn't all decent, Pat. There is crime and greed, the strong walking over the weak, and I do not intend to be walked over by Frank Pease. Twin R is ours and we're going to fight for it with the law and what force we have to use."

She stood up bruskly and marched out of the room, angry with both men and showing it by the set of her shoulders. Phil Royer said in apology, "The way she was raised. I have always been opposed to unnecessary violence, even if you may not believe that since you've still got a bullet of mine in you. Well, what's your battle plan?"

58

"I thought I'd borrow from Ace's book, ride in at night to catch them asleep."

Royer looked doubtful. "Wouldn't they expect something of the sort and be ready for it?"

"Could be. But I'm hoping they don't know about your loan and with the bank account frozen will be a little over-confident. A surprise could put you back in possession quickly and we could fight from strength."

"Damn it." Royer got up and prowled the room restlessly. "I feel helpless. I wear a gun but I'm no professional and I don't like having to depend on anybody else to do my fighting."

Wallace said quietly, "Everybody has to depend sometimes. I'm going to depend on you for an act. I suspect Pease has Spangler Cooper watching you for any sign of fight and I don't want him to see any. That's why I slipped up the back way, to keep him from suspecting until we're ready to hit them."

That did not make Phil Royer any happier and he kicked at a table leg. "Duck around corners like a spineless wonder. A fine showing that's going to be. Dork, do you think I'm a coward?"

"I think you're smart enough to weigh odds, and until Bucko's people get here they're all against you. Just hang loose until then."

Wallace left Royer and went down to spend the day on the hotel porch looking as idle as he could. At supper that night he made a point of ignoring the Royers and afterward wandered down to the Mermaid when he saw Spangler Cooper go there.

He allowed half an hour so it would not appear an intentional meeting, then entered casually and was pleased to find an empty chair at the table where the lawyer was playing poker, dropping into it with a nod to the others. The lawyer sounded unctious. "You still out of a job, Wallace?"

Dork raised and dropped his shoulders. "Not many jobs around with everybody on roundup. I'll wait a few more days and if nothing turns up I'll head east."

Cooper said in the same tone, "I might get Frank Pease to take you back. Now that he has to oversee the operation of two ranches . . ."

"What's that?" Dork Wallace sounded convincingly surprised.

"You knew Phil Royer's niece came up from Mexico to claim her ranch. Pease is helping out, putting a crew together to work it and chances are he'd let you have the foreman's spot there."

Dork studied the cards he was dealt and made a small bet. "I'd have to think about that. We've tangled too many times."

"Don't think too long. He'll have to have someone in a couple of days."

He stopped talking and the game went on, the players speculating what Phil Royer would do, whether swallow his pride and look for a local job himself or tuck in his tail and leave the country. Those who had seen the niece from Mexico had comments on her looks and jokes about who might step into a soft spot by marrying her. Her arrival and Royer's upset made for lively gossip that Wallace kept out of.

Shortly after midnight Wallace heard horses in the street and moments later Bucko Sollars batted the louvered doors apart, came in, put his back against the front wall and gave the room a slow, thorough appraisal. Someone said in a hoarse whisper that carried, "It's Bucko Sollars . . ."

A dead silence fell and all activity froze. Sollars swaggered to the bar and ordered whiskey. The poker game was forgotten. Movement began again as men edged toward the doors. The table emptied until only Wallace and Spangler Cooper were left and Cooper said in a tense undertone, "Wonder what he's doing here so far out of his territory."

"Who knows? Maybe it got hot for him." Wallace stood up and joined the wary retreat from the saloon.

On the dark street he walked unhurriedly to the livery where the hostler was snoring on his cot in the dingy office. Dork did not wake him. He went along the runway to the end stall where he had left his saddled horse earlier, mounted and rode out beside the corral at the rear to wait. Soon Sollars' animal brought the outlaw up the black alley and stopped beside Wallace. Dork said, "Where are the others?"

"Went on through town. We'll pick them up on the road. Let's go."

They walked the horses to the end of the alley, returned to the street where the row of buildings ended and continued beyond the outskirts. In a depression where the road dipped they found the nine riders.

"I want a quick fire," Wallace said. "Enough to light your faces so I can recognize you."

Sollars rumbled, "And so I can count that advance I got coming now."

A brush fire was built and they crouched around it, ugly, hard-eyed, thin-mouthed men who stared back at Dork, measuring him as he measured them. They were what he needed and perhaps more than that. He would have his job cut out to stay on top of them. He got names that would not be their original ones and as the flames dwindled he handed the five hundred dollars to Bucko Sollars.

Then they mounted again and rode cross country on a shortcut to the Twin R ranch headquarters.

CHAPTER
SIX

They crossed onto the Twin R well before dawn. Dork Wallace took his ten men within half a mile of the headquarters buildings and from a rise pointed out the cluster just visible on the open plain, the main house hidden under cottonwoods. He sent them on a detour to come in from the rear, left his horse for them to bring up, and went along the lane afoot to reconnoiter.

No dog gave an alarm. He angled toward the far corner of the corral, edged along the poles until he could make out the guards posted there, then his mouth set. There were two, one sitting with his back against the fence, the other stretched on the ground, and both asleep. Unless Frank Pease had hired new hands to occupy this ranch these were men he had commanded. They would have been thrown off the Lazy P for a lapse like this.

He left them as they were, counted ten horses within the fence, walked on among the dark buildings and met Sollars' crew behind the bunkhouse. They were all on foot now, the horses picketed where a whinney would not betray the raiders. Wallace deployed three to watch the side and rear windows from the outside and took the rest to the front door, easing that open.

The room was large, with sleeping space for a crew of twenty, but knowing Phil Royer's people were all away on roundup Pease had brought only a few here. Holding high the lantern he had lit outside Wallace stepped through, stood aside to let the others in. They crossed quietly to the bunks and at Sollars' signal hauled the six riders sleeping there to the floor. They were not gentle. The Lazy P sprawled on the boards, rolled to sit up, still stupefied, coming out of sleep. They looked into the barrels aimed on them and made no resistance.

Bucko Sollars' chuckle was a low thunder as he collected the holsters from the pegs in the bunk supports, slung them on the round table the crew used for poker. The Lazy P watched in stunned silence until they spotted Dork Wallace's face deep in shadow under his hat brim beneath the lantern above his head.

They gaped as the meaning hit them. Until so few days ago Dork had been their foreman on the Pease ranch. Now he was here with Bucko Sollars. They knew who Sollars was. The whole length of the Rio Grande valley knew, a bully on the edge of the law whom the Rangers had not yet come down on.

Bent Bentley, Wallace's top hand at Lazy P, who had always taken over as acting foreman when Dork was "fired," flushed to a dull red beneath his sunburn. "What the hell . . . Dork, what is this?"

Wallace did not explain. He said sharply that they were to dress, collect their gear, leave the Royer range, and not come back. "My advice," he finished, "clear out of the country for good."

They had taken Wallace's orders a long time. Shrugging, Bentley got to his feet, began making up his war bag and the others followed his lead without argument.

Dork told Sollars, "You handle this." He lifted his voice a little. "Steel, Black, come to the corral with me. Two guards there."

He left the lantern on the table, stepped out with the pair, and paused to adjust his eyes to the night before he went on. A few steps ahead of the others Dork reached the guard who lay full length, bent to take the rifle from the hand. His fingers were around the stock when a man behind him stumbled, swore. The instinct of danger made the prone man roll, wrenching the rifle with him, come up swinging the barrel at the head above him.

Dork dodged, caught the barrel, but before he could twist it free the other guard propped against the fence waked, pushed against the post for leverage and came up in a lunge onto Wallace's back. Long arms flung around Wallace and crushed him close to his body, broke his grip on the gun. The man on the ground swung the barrel hard against Dork's head. For the moment Dork was paralyzed, helpless.

From near him either Steel or Black fired into the chest of the guard as he pulled back for a second blow and the other Sollars man clubbed the ribs of the man on Wallace's back hard enough to break him loose, wrapped both hands in the collar, wheeled, and threw him at the corral poles. He sprawled through, landed on his buttocks and even as he landed drew his gun and snapped a shot that caught the man who had thrown him. Then he rolled to his feet and disappeared among the panicked, whirling horses.

It was Steel who went after him. Wallace had a glimpse of the ugly face as the man rushed by him. He did not yet have breath enough to call. He had just got his feet under him solidly when a third shot split the waning night. Dork Wallace drew his lungs full. Perhaps the killings had been necessary, Pease's was a hardcase crew, but if these two had worked under him he wished they had been taken alive and sent off with the bunkhouse riders. He sucked his teeth dry, scratched a match across them, looked at the face turned up at his feet. With a shock he recognized Clem Rafferty, one of the brothers who had tormented Pat Royer, of the clan who had a grudge against her father and whom Pease must have hired on because of that. The other guard then would be Clem's brother Rafe. It took the edge off his dissatisfaction. Still, he had hoped this would be a bloodless coup.

Running feet crossed the yard toward him, the six from the bunkhouse with Sollars' people on their heels, speeded by the gunfire. They gathered around the body with an angry murmur until other matches showed who it was, then they quieted down. None of them had any use for the Rafferty clan. The matches also lighted Wallace's face.

A high shriek at the rear of the circle sent the Sollars group in a crouching spin. The Lazy P did not react, well used to the sound. The shadow of a short, spindly scarecrow in a long nightshirt danced from one bare foot to the other sweeping a shotgun back and forth to cover them all. Frank Pease's piercing words were hard on the ears.

"Dork Wallace, what the hell you think you're doing? Boys, throw him off this place pronto."

The only move his crew made was to split, back away, leave a path between the rancher and his recent foreman, Bent Bentley growling that they had no guns. Pease cursed him, steadied his shotgun on Wallace, ten feet away, shouting, "Git, you, before I lose my patience. Off my place."

Dork Wallace stood very still. He was too far away to take the gun and in the excitement of this surprise the old man could be tipped over the edge to murder. He could not guess which would trigger a shot, his keeping silent or saying what had to be said. He chose silence.

There was a moment while Pease all but blew fire through his nose, then the shotgun veered, centered on Bucko Sollars as the biggest target in sight and Pease yelled.

"This scattergun can knock half of you over before one of you could draw. You like living, do like I say."

A welling of admiration filled Dork Wallace for this crazy bantam. He had been through many tantrums, many showdowns with old Ace Pease but this was the first time he had ever seen him stand up all alone against a short dozen armed men. He had a quick vista back through the years, a better understanding of how this shriveled gnome had clawed a way up through far taller, brawnier beings to become so dominant. It hit suddenly, the hurt that he was now committed to the opposite side. He wavered, tempted to once again yield to the fierce power that had drawn him back time after time.

A shadow moved at Pease's rear. Wallace almost called a warning. Then Steel's hand slammed around the rancher, grabbed the twin barrels, pushed them down. The double shot exploded into the ground. Released as though some field of energy around him had been shut off Wallace jumped the ten feet. He heard Pease's angry yelp, "Gimme that," then as Steel wrenched the gun away, turning Pease with him, Dork was behind the little figure, catching the wrists, swinging them against Pease's back, holding them fast. His calm flowed back. He said quietly, "Ace, quit this. Twin R is not your ranch."

Ann Royer's voice was cold. "No. It is mine and he is my manager."

Wallace had not heard her come. He turned his head and in the growing false dawn saw her, a robe gathered around her, her long blond hair in thick braids hanging across her shoulders halfway down her thighs. Vulnerable was the word that came, easy to hurt, and she had been hurt aplenty. Abruptly he was aware of the bold eyes that fastened on her, Bucko Sollars' in particular. Keeping his hold on Pease who had quit fighting him when he saw the girl from Mexico, he gave his order.

"Lazy P, saddle and ride out. Sollars, shove them west to Devils Creek, that's Twin R's line, then come back here and bury the dead."

Frank Pease had the sense to keep quiet while the horses were saddled. Sollars' crew appropriated them, herding the Lazy P on foot back to where they had left their animals. When they had gone Wallace began marching the rancher toward the house, telling him, "When you're dressed you're free to leave. Ann is welcome to stay. Phil will take care of her."

Walking rigidly at the rancher's side the girl said, "Mr. Pease, isn't there any law here? Will it let my uncle and these . . . thugs . . . put us off a ranch that is legally mine?"

Pease grunted. To Wallace it was a warning that the Lazy P owner was not through by a long sight. To forestall another grab Dork said mildly, "There's Texas law, ma'am. Taken from the Spanish. It says a woman's property needs a man to protect it, her nearest male relative. Since you aren't married that means Phil Royer will have the say as to who runs Twin R, and believe me it will not be Frank Pease."

She stopped, stunned, then ran to catch up, gasping, "Are you sure? Do you mean I am to be at the mercy of the man who stole my inheritance? I don't believe you."

"One way to find out," Dork told her. "Ask Spangler Cooper. I'm surprised he didn't tell you earlier."

Pease ground his teeth. "Didn't tell us because you just made up that law a minute ago. Go get your clothes on, little girl. We'll find out what the real law says."

Inside the house Dork Wallace stayed with Frank Pease while he dressed, watchful that the man did not add a gun to the outfit. When the girl came down from the second floor ready to ride, large eyed and white faced, he saw them to the corral, saddled for her while Pease vented his anger in jerking his cinch strap tight, watched them off at a hell bent run, then went for his own animal and turned it toward Del Rio after them. He smiled at the morning. It would be good to see this courageous blonde receive what was apparently her right, title to the ranch, and have the holding safe from Pease's grabbing hands, held and controlled for her by Phil Royer. Phil, he thought, was big enough to accept the change and make Ann welcome under the shelter of his strength.

CHAPTER
SEVEN

Bent Bentley had elected to take his five remaining riders to Del Rio rather than the home place. That was neutral territory. They all needed new hardware and belts if old man Pease intended to move against Twin R again, as Bentley was sure he did, and they could ride to Lazy P when they were armed afresh. He could not understand Dork Wallace turning on his old boss this way, particularly when the pretty girl from Mexico needed help, and curiosity ate at him.

He and the boys were still in town when the whirlwind arrived, Ace Pease and the blonde riding in as if the devil was right behind. The rancher spotted Bentley, flung down, threw the reins of both horses at him, bit out an order to take them to Thorngood's livery, and with the girl's arm tight in his claw stamped past the feed store and up Spangler Cooper's dusty outside stairway, cursing a steady stream. It did make a man wonder just what was going on.

Looking down from his window the lawyer also wondered. Cooper never expected such amenities as a handshake from Pease, but neither did he expect the storm that broke over him when the old man burst through the door ahead of the girl and yelled at him.

71

"Dork Wallace and Bucko Sollars and their riffraff booted us off Twin R. Wallace claims a woman in Texas ain't got no rights in handling her property, she has to have a man relative run it. Is that so or not?"

It was a blow to Spangler Cooper's solar plexis. Automatically he bent over Ann Royer's hand, seated her, then sank into his swivel chair, collecting his thoughts. He had hoped that Pease, Wallace, Phil Royer, none of them Texans, would not know of the old statute. It had been his intention to quietly court the girl from Mexico, marry her himself, and so come into control of the second largest ranch in the valley. Now there was no time for that leisurely approach. His lips thinned out.

"It's so. But I didn't think Wallace would know it. Her husband or closest male relation is responsible, so Phil Royer is her legal guardian. Until she marries. Miss Royer, purely to see justice done you, may I offer myself to become your husband to assure that you come into your rightful heritage? I am confident that together we could keep Twin R the prosperous property it is, and see it grow."

The blond girl's eyes widened, then narrowed in thought. She opened her mouth but before she could speak Ace Pease was shouting again at Cooper.

"Why you damn sneak. You're no better than this little orphan's uncle, wanting to steal everything she's got left in this world for yourself, and you don't even know the fine points of ranching. No sir, Annie, don't you listen to this snake, you listen to me. I'll . . ."

Pease was on the point of running a stampede. Plainly the girl needed a husband, and in a hurry, so she didn't have time to be choosy about the man. If she had let him finish he was certain he could have talked her into marrying him, old as he was, as a straight business proposition.

But she interrupted, saying in a faraway voice, "I'm listening. To both of you. Should it make me vain to be fought over this way by two such unselfish gentlemen? Lawsy me," she affected a deep South accent, "y'all make me feel a most desirable young lady. But I'll thank you to let me choose my own husband. After I think on it awhile."

"Think good," Pease growled. "Just keep in the front of your head what's at stake in who you pick."

Silkily the lawyer pressed his case, that he could defend her against any legal attacks Phil Royer might launch, that he had a southern background similar to hers, and inferred that he was young enough, cultured enough, presentable enough that they could have a harmonious union in which love could develop. Ace Pease broke in again and again with his arguments that what she needed most was a man with the experience to protect her holdings. She listened to all they had to say, her hands folded in her lap and her eyes on them. After an hour of it she drew a deep sigh, stood up, walked slowly to the window and looked down on the street.

On his way to Del Rio Dork Wallace met Bucko Sollars' band heading back to Twin R, laughing and pleased with themselves.

"Them Lazy P riders was bright red in the face, slinking into town like kicked curs with nothing on their hips and having to own up that they all needed new hardware. I don't figure they'll stay around with the hurrahing they'll take. And old Pease and his gal rode way around us, gave us a wide berth when we went by them. Looks to me like this was a dinky little chore we come so far to do."

Wallace eased himself in his saddle, building a smoke, saying evenly, "Don't get too cocky yet, Bucko. It isn't finished. Ace Pease won't give up this easy, so you're still on the job. I'm going in to tell Phil Royer and his daughter they can go home. You go on, bury the two Raffertys, then go locate the roundup and Tom Foster. Tell him as soon as the gather is complete to haze the Twin R stock back to the ranch. We'll cut out the shes and the unweaned calves and ship the rest. If Spangler Cooper tries to tie Royer up in court I want Phil in the best cash position possible. Then we'll sit and watch for Pease's next move. You've already been paid for two weeks and my bet is you'll make more."

The big man did not like the new orders, the prospect of idling on the isolated ranch for an indefinite time. With money burning his pocket he would rather be close to the saloons until it was gone. His laughter gone he rode on, grumbling under his breath.

Wallace continued into town, rode the length of the main street without seeing any of the Lazy P crew. At the livery he told the hostler to put his horse in a stall, leave it saddled, that he would want it again soon. Then he walked toward the hotel. He had one foot on the first step when his name was called from down the street. Turning toward the voice he saw Ann Royer come quickly down the last treads of Spangler Cooper's stairs and hurry toward him. He waited as he was until she came up, climbing above him to put their faces on a level.

"Dork Wallace," she said, "I ought to be angry with you, but I'm not. You only did what you thought was right." Her eyes this close to his were dark, troubled, her voice held deep pleading. "You tried to warn me about Frank Pease, how he would try to take my ranch away from me, and I didn't believe you. He sounded so sincere. Now I know, and I need your help."

He smiled at her. It was hard not to smile at a girl with her looks, especially when she admitted a mistake and turned to him in her trouble.

"Glad you found out in time and I'll do what I can, but you needn't worry. Your uncle is a good man, he'll look out for you. He just had a shock but he'll get over that."

The trouble deepened in her face and she shook her head, the morning sunlight dancing in her hair. "Oh no, he's not good, Dork. You should have heard him and my dear cousin, the way they talked when I first went to the ranch. They hate me. If I stayed there with them I'd be like an unwanted stepchild. Now I'm really alone. Listen to this. I've spent the morning between Frank Pease and Spangler Cooper and do you know what they're trying to make me do? Each of them wants me to marry him. They've been bickering over me as though I were something on an auction block. All they want is my ranch. Isn't there anybody I can trust?"

He had to laugh, the picture was so plain, the cunning lawyer and the greedy rancher reaching for her fortune. Ace Pease could have no other interest in her but Cooper would be stalking a handsome bride as well.

He sobered and said, "I'm sure there is, Ann, and any man would be proud to marry you even if you had nothing. I . . ."

The tears came without warning, filling the eyes to a shimmering brilliance and flooding out, down the cheeks. She shook them away with a sideways swing of her head. Wallace had one full look at them before her arms flung around his neck, her firm lips brushed his face and pressed hard against his mouth in a salt-tasting kiss. In her sudden move she lost her balance, began a sharp sideways fall. He caught her just in time, holding her to steady herself and longer than necessary in a reflex embrace. A tingling shock swept through him. Before he recovered she bent backward, drawing her hands forward to cup his cheeks, showing him a happy, tremulous smile, gasping aloud.

"It had to be you . . . I knew it . . . we can be married right away. Oh, Dork, it's perfect."

Emotions hit him like sheet lightning. He had never been in love and he knew this was not that, but he was jolted to his feet. And he would have been less than a ranch man if the Twin R did not flash to his mind.

He had not seen the screen door open, Patricia Royer start out and stop short as she saw the pair holding each other. He did hear the slam and had a glimpse of her skirt swirling away. It was like ice water thrown on him. The spell broke.

He let go of the girl, kept only one hand, towed her to a porch chair and pressed her into it, then crouched before her, his voice still not quite steady.

"Ann, I wasn't suggesting marriage. This is no way to choose a husband . . . or a wife. We don't know each other. We're strangers. Don't do a foolish thing like this. Wait until you find someone you know you want."

Her lower lip trembled. "You don't want me? Even if it would give you that beautiful ranch to manage? Dork . . . Dork . . . Could anyone else keep Frank Pease from overrunning it now that he has come so close to having it? Oh . . . what am I to do?"

Dork Wallace felt guilty. It was a new experience and it made him mad. Sure the kid felt abused and afraid, he didn't blame her for that with as little as she knew about her uncle, but didn't she realize the spot she was putting him on? He said more roughly, "Do what you should do. Make your peace with Phil Royer and between us we'll see that Ace doesn't move one inch onto Twin R. I'm going to see him now. I'll take you with me and prove what I've been saying."

She caught both chair arms so tightly her knuckles showed white. "No, no. Just go away and leave me alone. You make me feel as cheap as a bordello woman."

Living on Ace Pease's all-male Lazy P ever since his adolescence, the girls at Big Lizzie's house were the only kind he had known. He had never thought of them as cheap. They had to live and in raw Texas there were very few ways for single females to make a living. Wallace stood up abruptly, strode into the lobby, and slammed the screen as hard as Pat had moments ago. Let Ann Royer find out for herself what choices she had. Or maybe he could get Phil to talk to her, reassure her. He was still mad when he pounded on Royer's door and called his name.

For the second time in less than two minutes a girl's voice said, "Go away. Leave us alone."

Dork Wallace blinked, took a backward step, took off his hat, and scratched at his scalp with his little finger. Then his laughter erupted, the low chuckle rumbling up from deep within him. Through it his words had a jerkiness.

"Phil, don't you want to hear that you can go home now?"

Again Pat answered, sharp and bitter. "To live with you and my cousin? No thank you."

The parallel between this and Ann Royer's stubbornness grew funnier to Wallace. Pat Royer must have not only seen the kiss but heard her cousin's talk of marriage, but of course she had missed the rest of the conversation. He said with more emphasis, "No, Pat. You should have stayed in the doorway longer. Open up and let me straighten this out."

"We don't listen to double-crossing opportunists. You are fired and that's that."

But the door swung inward. Phil Royer towered in the opening, his face bleak as when he had looked at Wallace while Dork worked for Pease. Beyond him

78

Dork saw Patricia fling across the room, stop with her back to it at the window and stand rigid, her hands clenched around her folded arms. Royer waited, saying nothing. Wallace stood easy, hipshot, with a half smile.

"Misunderstanding downstairs. I got proposed to but I didn't buy." With a wicked mischief he added for Pat's benefit, "Seems a shame though. Easiest way to come by a ranch I ever heard of, but I'm not ready to marry anybody. Phil, she was panicked. Both Ace and Cooper had had her between them trying to browbeat her into marrying one of them. I've been telling her you'd look after her interests better than anyone but she's still spooked, thinks you deliberately cheated her. She'll come around. Right now I have a crew on Twin R and the house is waiting for you. I'll go for horses while you get ready."

Royer's face relaxed as Wallace talked, even to a fleeting twitch of his lips at Dork's jibe for his daughter, and at last he said in almost a whisper, "I guess we all learn about women the hard way. We'll be down by the time you get back."

"Seems I've got a way to go," Dork confessed and turned back toward the stairs.

He came onto the porch noting that Ann Royer still sat in the chair, turned away, head low and shoulders hunched, convulsing. He took one step toward her, then stopped. Bucko Sollars was running his big horse up the street. To Wallace that spelled trouble at the Twin R. He dropped down to the sidewalk, lifting his hand to signal he was there and as Sollars wheeled in said tightly, "What's wrong?"

Sollars' grin was wide. "Not a damned thing."

"Then what are you doing in town? I warned you Lazy P might try another grab."

The man sat arrogant, built himself a cigarette, and lit it before he grumbled, "They won't get far. I got nine men out there a regiment of cavalry couldn't move off. But they're bored and thirsty. Old man Royer didn't have nothing but a couple jugs of brandy and that's too sweet. I come in for a supply."

Wallace's tone tightened. Sollars was under orders to guard the ranch and this was a flagrant breach of discipline, an indication that Dork could not trust these men if he should need them again. He regretted Bent Bentley and the old crew he had been able to rely on.

"Get it then," he said shortly. "Then go back to your job. Be there when I bring the Royers out."

Sollars grunted, flicked his reins, and rode on toward the saloon. Wallace turned the other way, forgetting the girl on the porch, fretting over what to do about Sollars. At the livery he rented horses for the Royers, who had ridden the buckboard when Pease drove them out of Twin R. When they were saddled he mounted and led them to the hotel. Phil and Patricia Royer were on the porch, trying to talk to the girl from Mexico but her hands were tight over her ears and she did not raise her head. They gave up and came down to the horses, looking troubled and perplexed. Pat mounted without looking at Dork, her face flushed with embarrassment, and he did not press her. Phil said nothing, his mind on the difficult niece. They left Del Rio in a strained silence.

CHAPTER
EIGHT

Three people watched with particular interest as they rode out. On the hotel porch the girl from Mexico turned off her tears and chewed her lip, wondering how deeply involved Dork Wallace was with Patricia Royer, if that was why he had been so quick to turn his back on what instinct told her was a vastly tempting offer. She knew she was beautiful, much more so than Patricia whose most exciting feature was the unusual, wide-spaced pale eyes, and men had been after her since she was thirteen. Coupled with control of the big ranch, with her display of helplessness when Wallace left the hotel, she could not see how he could have resisted. She shrugged. Young, big, capable, Dork Wallace as a husband would have been the solution of her choice but he was not all important.

Bucko Sollars watched resentfully over the batwing doors of the Mermaid bar.

Frank Pease looked down from Cooper's window with bright, birdlike attention. He had been there ever since Ann Royer had turned away from the same window and gone flying down the stairs to waylay Dork Wallace. Marrying her himself would have been best but if she could grab off Wallace that would be all right.

He could manage Wallace, always had, and Dork was the best possible man he could have on Twin R. But plainly Dork had turned down the offer. That had made Pease nervous until Bucko Sollars rode in, went to the saloon and was still there.

Pease left the lawyer's office without a parting word when Wallace and the Royers were out of sight and headed for the Mermaid. At that time of day only one bartender was behind the counter and Sollars was the only customer, a bottle and glass in front of him, his big face surly, reflected in the mirror. In that he saw Pease come in and cross to his side and watched him without turning his head.

Pease, too, looked at the mirror and kept his voice low. "I want to talk to you."

"Talk."

"Over at the corner table."

Sollars took his bottle and glass, moving without hurry to the table. Pease signaled for a glass, went to sit opposite Sollars, and without invitation poured himself a drink, saying, "I'll buy."

"Yep. What are you after?"

Still in a low tone Pease was direct. "What will you take to clear off Twin R and stay off?"

Sollars studied the whiskey in his glass as if the answer lay in there, then rumbled, "Why? Royer's got legal control until his niece catches a man."

"That don't concern you a bit. I'm going to have that ranch. How much?"

Sollars shrugged. He had considered kidnaping Ann Royer, marrying her himself, then backed off from the

82

idea. He did not like cattle, did not want a continuing responsibility for land, did not want to be tied to one place or one woman.

"Five thousand."

Frank Pease yelped in outrage and hissed, "You damn robber. Royer can't be paying you more than one."

The huge man grinned. He was already burned at the way Dork Wallace had thrown orders at him as if he were a common cowhand and here was his chance to get back at the man.

"One a month," he said, "and Wallace promised us several months. I mean to collect one way or another."

The old rancher poured and swallowed a second drink. "I'll give you two, and nothing to do for it but ride out."

Bucko Sollars' eyes narrowed to slits and his voice came ugly. "Maybe you didn't hear me."

Frank Pease was old at the ways of dickering. He shoved back his chair, grunted in disgust, spun up, and started for the door. He had reached it, was slapping it apart when Sollars called for him to wait. Pease stopped, one hand on the shuttered panels but did not look back. He heard Sollars' boots cross the floor, then the low words close behind him.

"I'll come down to four."

"Two, I said. I wouldn't pay four to see the devil hop over the moon." He shoved the doors apart and took another step.

Sollars' whiskey breath was sour on Pease's cheek as he sneered. "Bad as you want that ranch you're plenty hard to do business with, but I'll meet you halfway."

"All right, three."

"Now."

Pease turned then, affecting a hurt expression. "You don't trust my word?"

Sollars' grin was wolfish. "Nobody does. We walk down to the bank and get the cash or no deal."

Frank Pease knew he was licked on this. Sollars poked his back with four fingers, pushed him through the door, followed him out. Wind channeled between the buildings whirled little dust devils ahead of them, filled their mouths with grit that matched Pease's irritation with the giant.

There was no one in the bank except Hyde Stewart who owned it, the teller being gone on an errand. He hid his surprise when Frank Pease withdrew three thousand dollars, hid his disapproval that Pease immediately handed the money to Sollars. He resented the rancher for his brigand's tactics and despised Bucko Sollars, but Pease was too rich and Sollars too dangerous for him to offend either. Knowing that some malicious bargain had been made, he wished Phil Royer and Dork Wallace were still in town, but he had seen them and Pat ride out half an hour before. It made him uneasy to think what Pease must be planning. He would have been more than uneasy if he had trailed them out, overheard their talk and the later development between Pease and the girl from Mexico.

On the sidewalk Sollars headed back toward the saloon for his horse, saying, "We'll be gone by sundown, you old thief, and the rest is up to you, whatever you got in that trick head."

"That's not what I want," Pease said quickly. "Ride on out to Twin R and act like you're still hired to Wallace until I get there tomorrow. Then we can both surprise him."

Sollars lifted and dropped his big shoulders and said, "I like that better. I want to see Wallace fold when you stick your pin in his balloon."

They separated at the hotel, Pease dropping off there where Ann Royer still sat weighing the decision she must make soon, knowing what it must be but revolted by the prospect. Pease lowered himself into the next chair with a pleased sigh.

"Girlee, I just bought me Bucko Sollars. He's changed sides and you'll owe me three thousand dollars when the ranch is yours. Now we only got one more step to take, to get us hitched up, and we got all afternoon to do it."

The blond girl squared around on him, sucking in a noisy breath as though getting ready to jump off a high cliff into turbulent water. Pease read it as a prelude to further stalling and was afraid she would turn to the tall, youthful, slick Spangler Cooper. He clamped his claw hand on her wrist and shook it, urgency flushing his face red.

"You know I'm the only help you're going to get here. Sure I'm old enough to be your grandfather, but that's in your favor too. I'm the richest man in this hunk of Texas and I got no kin at all. You'll have it, every mile and buck when I die."

Air seeped out slowly through her pursed, parted lips. With her free hand she patted the claw firmly, said evenly, "Yes, Frank. It will be good business for both of us."

He was on his feet, tugging her up, towing her to the slatted sidewalk and along it at a half run to the courthouse and Judge Lloyd Lindsay's chambers where the odor of leather-bound books drying out in the heat made the nose twitch.

"Lloyd," Pease cawed, "this is little Annie Royer and we come to have you marry us. Fetch your book and tie the knot tight."

Lindsay, florid beneath a long white mane that curled against his collar, looked the girl over from the crown of her head to her feet, and a corner of his thick mouth turned up. He had heard the talk in the saloons of Phil Royer's niece and her determination to put him off Twin R, but it amazed him that she would go so far as to take Frank Pease as husband. He knew what she would let herself in for. It turned his stomach.

He said tartly, "Ma'am, you'd better do some hard thinking before you give your promise to this old billy goat. He's apt to live a long time yet and you'll be mighty sorry."

Her chin went up and she matched his tone. "It is not intended as a love match. I must protect myself in the only way allowed in a state that claims women are too weak-minded to run their own lives. Do as Frank says."

Lindsay huffed with a flash of temper. The way she sounded she probably deserved what she was asking for. He barked at Pease that they would need two witnesses, then turned his chair, put his back to the girl while the rancher pranced off to round up Bent Bentley and another Lazy P rider from the bar nearest the livery.

It was as unwelcome a ceremony as the judge had performed since he began his practice. When they had gone he lifted a bottle from the bottom desk drawer, swilled whiskey around his mouth to wash away the taste of the words.

Frank Pease paraded his bride first to Spangler Cooper's office to crow. Cooper surrendered with outward grace and a mental shrug. A patient man, he would wait, develop a friendship with the girl and be ready in the wings for the time she would be widowed. The wry thought struck him that this might be very soon, that Phil Royer could well kill Frank Pease for his trickery.

The Lazy P crew was sent home to the ranch to help with the roundup there, then the couple had a wedding supper at the hotel, Pease celebrating until he was more than a little drunk. Ann left him at the table muttering, bragging to himself, locked herself in the room Pease had taken, and began undressing.

She had hung her blouse on a peg and was pulling her skirt over her head when the door rattled and Pease's slurred voice came through it demanding to be let in. The girl did not answer. Pease kicked the panel, waited a short moment, then yelled.

"Damn it, you're my wife. Do I have to shoot the lock off?"

She called, "Just a minute," dropped the skirt over her hips again and picked up the small revolver she had worn out of Mexico and still wore as a defense. With that in her right hand she unlocked the door and ran backward out of reach, then said, "Now you can come in."

Frank Pease pushed through, slammed the door behind him, stood swaying, his eyes out of focus, mumbling, "Hell of a note, lock a man out on his wedding night. Come here."

She stayed where she was, the gun raised on him, waggling it until he saw it and his jaw dropped, then said sharply, "Our marriage is a business arrangement. That's all it is. Don't try to touch me. If you come one step closer I will shoot you. In the stomach. It is not a quick or easy way to die."

Frank Pease was suddenly sober. Even a small gun could do much damage at this range and the girl's tone was clear warning. He looked at her as if he had not seen her before, then laughed.

"Why, gal, you're quite a wench, ain't you? We're gonna be a fit match, and don't you think I'm not still a man. You put that popgun down and I'll prove it."

"You heard me. Go get yourself another room. If you're not out of here in one minute I'll shoot."

With a grudging respect in his amazed voice the rancher told her, "Damned if I don't believe you would, honey. You've got real guts." He turned carefully and went back to the hall.

He walked toward the stairs debating, the whiskey taking hold again. He did not dare go to the Mermaid for more to drink and a poker game. He would be a laughing stock on this night in a room where he could not count a friend. It was his boast that he had no friends, that his small body cast a long shadow of fear unmatched by bigger men, of unwilling respect in a raw and hard society. He was too keyed up by the victories of the day to try to sleep this early but he did not want to be seen.

He slipped out through the hotel's rear door, took the alleys to the back of Big Lizzy's house and spent his wedding night as he had many, many in his bachelorhood.

CHAPTER
NINE

Bucko Sollars' man Steel sat perched in the upper branches of a big cottonwood where he had an overview of all the approaches to Twin R, and called down an all clear when Dork Wallace rode in with the Royers, whistled a shrill note as he saw Patricia. The whistle brought the other eight spilling from the bunkhouse expecting this was a signal of an attack. They stood around the doorway oggling the girl as she rode to the corral and dismounted. Wallace frowned at the behavior, and that he did not see Sollars among the men.

Phil Royer's mouth clamped tight. He resented needing this type on the place at all and he damned Ace Pease again, hurrying his daughter into the house.

Dork Wallace lingered to unsaddle the horses, then detoured to the bunkhouse. With the girl out of sight the men had gone back inside, returned to the poker game the whistle had interrupted, and ignored Wallace when he stepped into the doorway. He said nothing and did not stay. As long as they stayed here quietly they would start no trouble. He continued on to the house to advise Patricia to keep within the walls as long as the hardcase crew was around.

"You'd better stay here for supper," Phil Royer told him. "Keep as clear of that crowd as you can until a fight comes. What do you think is keeping Sollars?"

"Arrogance, I'd guess. Showing me he'll run his own show and be damned to the foreman. He'll turn up in his own time."

Royer led him to the room he used as an office and they talked about the ranch while the girl was busy in the kitchen. They heard Sollars ride in just as the Chinese cook beat a chow call on the triangle outside the cookshack. He was full of whiskey, bellowing for help to carry the bottles from his saddlebags into the bunkhouse, and stood at the window watching the transfer before the crew answered the supper call. Wallace did not go out. Food should take the edge off Sollars' liquor and he would wait until then before talking to him.

By the time supper was finished in the dining room Dork Wallace felt more at home than he ever had. At the Lazy P there had been no sense of belonging. Ace Pease ate with his crew but his treacherous temper made for an atmosphere of always being poised to jump. The food there had been mostly Mexican, heavy with chili, beans, tortillas, fried meat, thrown on a table covered with oilcloth.

Pat Royer spread white linen, served roast beef with baked potatoes, honey with light and fluffy biscuits instead of the sour dough he had grown up on, creamed onions, a hot dried apple pie and tea, a drink he had never before tasted and found surprisingly pleasant. He had not known any food could be this good and when at length he pushed away from the table he said, "I'd better not do this often or I'll be too fat to mount a horse. Let me help with the dishes to make up for it."

The girl started to refuse but Royer said, "Go to it while I catch up on some book work."

Wallace handled the china as if it were egg shells, carrying it to the kitchen, drying it as Pat washed. From the corner of her eye she noticed the gentle touch of the long, calloused fingers and smiled.

"You're new at this sort of job, Dork?"

A corner of his mouth turned up, mocking himself. "Only dishes I ever cleaned were tin ones we wiped out with sand on a trail drive. I never even saw any this thin."

"They're from England, Dad's wedding present to my mother. I know it isn't good manners in this country to ask a man where he's from, but you're not Texan, are you?"

"I don't mind telling you. I was born in New Orleans. My mother died then and my old man took another woman to raise me. He was a two-bit gambler and dragged us all over the West. When I was around eleven I couldn't take any more of either of them and cut out on my own, bumped into a drive Pease was making to Dodge City, hired on and stayed with him."

"All these years?" She sounded incredulous. "How could you put up with him?"

"Needed the job to begin with, then I got so I didn't pay any attention when he let off steam. When he made me foreman it was the best berth I knew of."

"But you finally did quit for good. What decided you?"

Wallace thought in silence for a long moment, then said slowly, "I can't really put my finger on that. Maybe because it galled me to know the old buzzard would find a way to beat your cousin out of this ranch. I didn't want to have anything to do with cheating her. She'd had enough happen to her already."

"Yes." Pat sounded distressed. "I'm so sorry for her. I do hope she changes her mind about Dad and comes to us. It would be nice to have another woman here to talk to. I like our men but they're not interested in some of the things I am."

That was an opening for a question to satisfy his own curiosity and he said idly, "I hadn't thought about you being lonely. Would that be why you called on the Princess the other day? You don't really believe her act, do you?"

She looked up at him with a strange, puzzled expression. "She amuses me, a change from listening to the Del Rio ladies talk clothes, babies, and food. But Dork, this is peculiar. That day she told me a stranger was coming soon who would make a big change in my life. At the time I thought she was thinking of a man, a romance. What if she meant Ann Royer? It gives me a creepy feeling now."

Wallace chuckled. "Coincidence. Fortune tellers are strong on predicting romances. It's bait to keep you coming back for more."

The cleanup was finished. The girl put things away then led Wallace to the parlor. Royer was already there, offering a cigar as Pat brought a tray with a bottle and three tiny glasses, pouring them full. Royer handed one to Dork, asking, "Do you like brandy?"

Dork's mocking smile warped up. "Like your tea, I never had brandy."

"I discovered a taste for it when I drove some cattle to New Orleans just after the war."

Dork tasted it, a smooth liquid with a faint fruit flavor that would take him time to appreciate, accustomed as he was to the raw whiskey of the West.

Royer sipped, then said, "How long would you think we have to keep Sollars here? When do you imagine Pease will give up?"

"Not until he knows he's whipped. He'll wait until the roundup is over, then probably hit us with his whole crew, and they're a lot rougher than your regular riders."

The rancher sighed. "What can he hope to do? If the ranch is Ann's what claim could he have? Well, we'll have to wait and see. Speaking of the roundup, I'm going out there in the morning. There's not much work needs doing here but you might keep the Sollars men busy mending the corral fence. Some of the posts are in bad shape."

Wallace did not comment. But Phil Royer still did not understand about the fighting crew. If he suggested fence mending they would tell him to go to hell. Tiredness washed him, both physical and mental as he thought ahead of the problem of keeping on top of the hired guns. He put the glass on the tray and dipped his head to the girl.

"Thanks for the best supper I ever had, and good night, both of you."

She flushed, embarrassed, telling him softly, "Come back for breakfast."

"I'll take you up on that before you change your mind."

Wallace left by the front door, stopped at the foot of the gallery steps to look for minutes at the brilliant glitter of stars that appeared to hang almost within reach, then crossed to the bunkhouse. The men were playing stud again, except Sollars who snored in his bunk, so his talk with the big man would have to wait for morning. Dork paused at the big table, watching the game. Steel was the heavy winner and now Jones was missing, presumably on guard. No one looked up, on one invited him into the game. A hostile chill shut him out. He was paying them but he was not of them, was not their lawless kind.

He went on to his bunk, stripped to his underwear, stretched out and pulled the light blanket over him. The years of living at Lazy P had trained him to sleep in spite of lamps and noise, but this was not a noisy room. The men here played poker tight-lipped and grim, as if survival depended on the cards.

He did not know how late they kept at it. When he waked before daylight they were in the bunks. He pulled his boots on, draped his clothes and belt over one arm and went out to the wash bench, took a towel from the stack there and the square of yellow soap and crossed the yard to the gully where a clear stream ran. Concealed at the bottom he stripped, waded waist deep and dived under the tepid water, then lathered his lean, corded body and his hair. Afterward he swam in the shallow pool, catfish sliding sluggishly away from his splashing. At Lazy P a bath once a week had been his habit, but if he was to eat with Pat Royer and her father he should go with a clean hide. On the bank again he toweled roughly in the cool early light, dressed, and climbed out of the gully.

There was already a lamp burning in the kitchen. Wallace crossed the yard, knocked on the door, and went in when the girl called. The smells of fresh boiled coffee and frying meat made him ravenous in spite of the big supper and Pat dancing between table and stove was a far better eye opener than the rheumatic grouch who cooked for Lazy P.

Spooning batter from a yellow bowl onto a sizzling griddle she tossed him a smile. "Coffee's ready, pour yourself a cup and sit down."

He poured, heard Phil Royer's boots in the hall, and filled a second cup and took both to the table to be out of the girl's way. Royer nodded without speaking, looking groggy as though he had not slept well, drinking deeply from the smoking cup. Patricia joined them with platters of meat and high piles of tender cakes, a pitcher of warm sorghum. Wallace passed up the meat to eat a dozen of the cakes awash in the sweet syrup, to the girl's amusement.

"You do know how to flatter the cooky, Dork."

"This isn't flattery," he told her. "Lazy P never saw a table like yours."

Phil Royer finished with more coffee, drinking it at the stove. "I ought to be home before dark but if I'm not don't wait supper on me. Pat, remember, keep out of sight of those mongrels. If you need anything from outside let Dork bring it. Wallace, watch over her."

When he had gone Dork again helped with the dishes, then went out to the yard. The kitchen was a separate wing at the back of the house with doors opposite each other. One opened toward the outbuildings and corral, the other on that part of the yard where a pile of wood lay in short chunks and beyond that the headframe of the well rose on top of a stone casing. Dork split wood, filled the firebox beside the kitchen range, and drew two buckets of water for the stove reservoir. Pat was not in the room, was making up beds he supposed or some housekeeping chore. After he had done all he could think of he started toward the bunkhouse.

Halfway there he stopped in midstep. Some of the horses were gone from the corral, about half of the fighting crew's remuda, though Bucko Sollars' heavy-chested bay was there. Moving faster he came against the door, slapped a palm against it, and slammed it open. Sollars was alone, at the table with his head in his hands, and jolted up at the sudden noise.

"Hell, man. My head's already split. You busted it wide open."

"I'll bust more than that." Wallace sounded furious. "Where are the men? Who's on watch?"

Sollars sagged back in the chair. "Ah . . . keep your shirt on. I'm on watch, and lousy as I feel I can wipe up that Pease outfit. The boys wanted to scout around, get the lay of the land so they wouldn't run onto a surprise if there's a running fight. Go bring some coffee over here."

Wallace hung his fingers over his gun butt, relaxed but ready. At best Sollars was a prickly customer and with a hangover he could be doubly mean.

"Go yourself. Get to the cookhouse and drink a whole pot. You might need a clear head any time."

At least the big man did not argue. If he had called a showdown and Wallace had had to shoot him the fat would have been in the fire. He would not have only Ace Pease to worry about but the bullies who followed Sollars. It had been a risk to jump the man but apparently the headache was bad enough to blunt his temper. Sollars got to his feet groaning and went out with heavy steps.

Dork Wallace was as mad as he had ever been. As usual when the normally even-tempered are struck with anger his rage made his stomach flutter. He needed hard physical labor to work off the spasms. He tramped to the tool shed for shovel and pick, then on beside the horse barn where new corral posts lay already cut, loaded several across a wheelbarrow and pushed it to the fence. Digging and wrenching, throwing his full strength against the wood he yanked out one dry rotted pole, replaced it and went to the next. Because it was cumbersome to work in he left his gun belt there. By midmorning he had calmed down. Sollars had not reappeared, nor had the men returned. When he heard horses in the lane he thought it would be them, but as they came into sight he saw only two riders, and could not distinguish them at the distance. Throwing down the shovel he walked to the yard to intercept them.

Incredibly they were Frank Pease and the girl from Mexico.

Behind Wallace a door slammed. Bucko Sollars came from the cookhouse, crossing to stand beside Dork as the pair rode up and reined in, dismounting. Wallace felt Sollars' presence rather than saw him as he watched the new arrivals impassively. Until today he had only seen Ann Royer in the riding trousers she had worn out of Mexico. Now she was even more striking in a long dress that matched her blue eyes as she met his, cold and accusing.

Frank Pease's grin had a warning smugness. "Phil around here?"

"Up with the roundup," Wallace said flatly. "His daughter's in the house. She's been hoping her cousin would come to live on Twin R."

"Just why I brought her out. Dork, you plain missed out all around. Catch up your gear and clear off. I'm firing you for the last time."

A new worry began to nag at Wallace, but he must play this game out and he said, "I'm not working for you, Ace. I'm Phil Royer's foreman."

"Not on this ranch you ain't." Pease wasn't shrieking and that was ominous. "Annie's got a husband now and Twin R is hers. The Royers are out."

Wallace knew before he asked. "Who married her?"

"Me. Come on in, honey, and we'll tell your cousin she's moving."

A coldness filled Dork Wallace. He had felt truly sorry for this orphaned girl in her plight. Now that was swept away by the bitter discovery that she would sell herself to such a man as Frank Pease for pure selfish greed, that she was stupid enough to believe Pease would not soon euchre her out of even title to the property.

They had already started for the house while he stood rooted in dismay. Then he thought of Pat, who should not have to face this pair alone, and strode past them, reached the front door first, went in without knocking and called to her.

She came from a rear room, a duster in her hand and her hair tied in a cloth, saw Ann just behind Wallace and opened her arms with a glad smile, hurrying forward. Wallace intercepted her, held one arm, saying quickly, "Keep back, Pat. She's here to claim the ranch. Pease says they're married."

Pat Royer stood very still, her eyes widening on Wallace, then turning to look the other girl up and down and finally settling on Pease, her face changing from pleasure at thinking her cousin was here as a family member to shock, then to open doubt.

"I'll need proof before I accept anything Frank Pease says." Her voice was faint but positive.

The girl from Mexico lifted her left hand slowly, palm down, exhibiting the bright gold ring. Pat Royer shook her head.

"Not enough. Anyone can wear a ring. Have you a certificate from the court?"

The old rancher shrugged. "It's being made up, but the record book's all signed by the judge. You can go look for yourself."

"No," Pat Royer stood fast. "You go. Bring the paper here when you have it. Until then I won't believe you."

Bucko Sollars had shoved in after Pease. "They're hitched all right. His foreman stood up with them and come in the saloon where I was to spread the news."

The rancher stepped away from the doorway. "Now that's settled, I want you two off this place in fifteen minutes. No. Wait up. The girl can go but I'm tired of Dork Wallace always butting in on me. Bucko, he's out here rustling cattle, ain't he? He needs a hanging."

Sollars' draw was fast. In the time it took him to make a step forward to knock Wallace out with the barrel Dork snapped, "You sold out."

"He upped the ante, chump." Sollars had the gun shoulder high.

Wallace missed the weapon he had left by the corral fence. He jumped, caught Sollars' wrist in both hands, twisting, forcing the arm to bend backward savagely until the fingers spread. The gun dropped at Pat Royer's feet. She snatched it up, cocking it, whipping it toward Frank Pease as he grabbed at his holster. He had sense enough to freeze without drawing. Ann Pease had slapped at her waist, but in changing to the dress she had left her little revolver in town.

Pat Royer's steady voice said, "You two go to the wall. Ann stand against it. Frank stand against her."

They had no doubt that this girl who was losing her home was mad enough to shoot, and moved carefully

101

to obey. Pat walked forward, the gun aimed at the rancher's middle, and with the muzzle against his shirt took his from his holster. Then she backed away, around Wallace and Sollars where they fought on the floor, Sollars with his huge frame having the best of it. He was astride Dork's back, one hand full of hair, beating Dork's head against the boards. Still holding Sollars' gun on Pease Pat bent, put the hard muzzle of the rancher's heavy weapon against Bucko's neck at the spine and shouted to be sure he heard.

"Stop it. Let go or I'll blow your head off."

The big outlaw opened his fingers, but he ducked aside, twisted, grabbing for her arm. She jumped out of reach, tripped, sat down hard, both guns exploding. The one that had been trained on Pease fired wild, into the ceiling. The other shot buried itself in the thick flesh of Sollars' leg. Bucko bawled, rolled, grabbed at the wound. Frank Pease lunged on Pat Royer, clawed at one gun. Before he could tear it away from her Dork Wallace was on his feet, lifting the little rancher by his collar and the seat of his pants and with the momentum of turning threw him against the wall beside Ann. As he came around he took one gun from Pat.

Pease's teeth rattled as he crashed but he came up, eyes wary on Pat where she sat with the second gun steady again, wiping blood from his mouth and shrieking now.

"Sollars, holler your crew in here fast."

Sollars rocked over his hurt leg and watched Wallace and the iron aimed at him, grating through clenched jaws, "They ain't here. I sent them off to be out of the

102

way. Quit your squalling and do something before I bleed to death."

Without sympathy Dork Wallace told the double-crossing giant, "Move over with your bride and groom where I can keep the three of you quiet." He waited while Sollars humped across the room on his buttocks, grimacing with every move, then took the gun Pat still held, saying, "I'll take you to your father as soon as you pack a trail bag and a grub sack. Bring whatever guns are in the house."

The girl got up and went immediately. Wallace liked her for not arguing, not wasting time on questions, for the courage with which she was now accepting this heavy blow. She was not gone long on her trip to the rear rooms, bringing back two made-up blanket rolls, taking them on to the corral, then returning to the kitchen.

Sollars' bullet had apparently cut a blood vessel and there was a fast growing spread on the floor. Wallace raised his voice to the girl.

"Bring a stick of kindling for a tourniquet before you pack the food."

She came with it and Wallace tossed it at Pease. The rancher used his neck handkerchief, twisting the stick in the cloth viciously, as if he enjoyed hurting the outlaw further because he had lost the fight with Dork. When Pat Royer appeared again dragging a heavy bag along the floor Wallace let her pass behind him, then backed toward the door. Bucko Sollars glowered at him, baring his teeth, blaming him for his hurt instead of the girl.

"I got a long memory, Wallace, and I'll find you wherever you go. You're a dead man right now."

Pease added, "Hear him good, Dork, because I'm going to offer five thousand dollars for the man who lays you by the heels."

Wallace's mouth thinned out in a tight line. "That's pretty strong talk from a pair looking down a muzzle. Ace, if I shoot you now I can make a widow out of that sorry excuse for a woman. The country would be better off if I shot all three of you."

The girl from Mexico clapped a hand against her mouth, gasping, hissing at Pease. "Frank . . . He's going to murder me."

Ace Pease sneered at Wallace. "No he ain't. He's too chicken livered. That's why he'll never amount to a damn. Only reason he was a good foreman over at Lazy P was because I stiffened up his backbone every step."

Wallace knew the truth of that. The men who succeeded in beating this enormous country were a ruthless breed while he could not bring himself to fire at an unarmed man even though leaving these three alive here could cost him his own life later. At the door he paused, shoved one gun under his belt and told them, "Stay right here until we ride out. Pat will be watching and she has the right to defend herself if you make any move."

He passed the gun to the girl on the porch, left her in the open doorway, slung the tote bag over his shoulder, detoured to the bunkhouse to roll his gear, then walked to the corral. He saddled two horses, loaded the rolls and grub sack on a third, fanned the others out and away, buckled on his belt, and as he led the string across the yard drove the two Pease animals off. At the porch he mounted, drew his own gun and held it on the door until Pat had come down and was in her saddle. They rode out at an easy pace. With no arms left in the house and no mounts, they would not be followed for some time.

Pat Royer sat straight backed. She did not once look behind her. They headed northwest toward the roundup, silent for half a mile, then the girl said quietly, "I left bandages and salve on the kitchen table but Sollars needs a doctor. Should we have left a horse for him?"

Dork Wallace gave her a warped smile. With all they had done to her she could return good for their evil. "The tourniquet will keep him alive, I'm afraid, and Ace can sweat a little catching up an animal. Forget them."

CHAPTER
TEN

At Devil's Creek they stopped for a midday meal. Dork Wallace built a quick greasewood fire on the bank, filled the coffeepot and canteens from the stream, let the horses drink and tied them. Pat Royer sliced side meat in the fry pan, split cold biscuits to warm in the grease as it rendered out, pounded coffee beans on a flat rock and put a handful in the pot when it boiled, setting it aside to steep. They ate unhurried, giving the animals an hour's rest. Pat scrubbed the tin dishes and pan with sand in the streambed while Dork killed the embers, pouring the leftover coffee on them until they quit sizzling. Then they rode again.

Both watched the horizon and the land between for Sollars' crew, not knowing whether they were in on the sellout, but they saw no one until evening when they found the roundup camp. It was dusty, busy, noisy as the big combined crews hazed stock to branding fires and separated the animals to be driven to the railroad from those to be left on the range. Lazy P was there, keeping to its own fire, distant from the Twin R people. Pat and Dork circled the bawling gather until they located Royer's men, saw the rancher squatted by their blaze with a coffee cup. He got up as his daughter and foreman rode in, saluting them with a wave, saying when they stepped down, "When I saw Pease's crew here I thought I'd better stay and see that our calves had the right brand run on them. What brought you?"

Before answering Dork Wallace asked, "Are any of Bucko Sollars' people around?"

"Haven't seen them. Aren't they at the ranch?"

"No. Sollars must have sent them back to Eagle Pass. Phil, there's bad news. He sold us out to Pease and Ann married Ace. They're grabbing Twin R. Pat brought you some clothes and what money was there because you can't go back there."

The big rancher's face lost all color. "Why, that rotten scoundrel. What kind of creature can that niece of mine be? Marry Frank Pease? I didn't think even he would go that far. What kind of animal is he?"

"The kind," Pat Royer said, "who would order Bucko Sollars to hang Dork Wallace and, when I shot Sollars in the leg said he would offer five thousand for Dork's scalp."

Wallace waited for the man to absorb that, saw Royer's mouth drop open and the disbelief in his eyes change to a stubborn glitter, then he forestalled the decision he read in the hardening eyes.

"Ace will make the same offer for you, and Sollars' hardcases will go for it. It will be healthier if you and Pat go far away from this territory where you won't be bushwhacked, because Pease won't feel secure about Twin R until you're dead. The way he thinks he'll be sure you'll try to kill him."

The rancher appeared to swell with his growing anger. "And by God that I will. I am not going to let him get away with any of these tricks and threats."

Dork said with deliberate casualness, "Kill Ace and you'll put Pat in danger. Your niece is cold blooded enough to have her murdered as well as you."

Phil Royer's full attention swung to his daughter. "Do you believe that, Pat? What's your instinct about her?"

"After watching her this morning I'm sure she would. I don't believe there's anything she wouldn't stoop to to hold Twin R. Dad, we have to write off the ranch and go somewhere else."

The man studied her for a long, thoughtful time while he made his choice. In the end his shoulders sagged with the defeat he finally admitted. His voice was unsteady.

"In that case we'd best go to my cousin Randal's spread in the Big Bend. He might help us re-establish down there. I'll pay off the crew tonight. We'll start in the morning."

Wallace cut in. "You'd better start now, ride the night. Sollars will do that and you need as much lead as you can get."

Pat Royer asked, "And you, Dork?"

"I'll drift on."

Phil Royer turned back to Wallace. "Why don't you throw in with us? I'll need a foreman down south when I find a place."

Dork Wallace's smile came. He had hoped for this, to stay with these people, a man he admired and the girl he was more and more drawn to as her strength and capabilities were shown to him. Agreeing, trying not to sound too eager, he walked with Royer to the chuckwagon where the Twin R crew had gathered to wait for supper, stretched on the trampled ground or hunkered against the wheels.

Royer had with him the money Pat had brought from the house. He stood over the men, telling them in a bleak, controlled tone, "I'm paying you off and saying good-by, boys. Ace Pease and Ann Royer, my niece from Mexico, took the ranch away from me, so the jobs are gone. I'm leaving the valley."

There was a stunned silence that dragged out to embarrassment. Bo Short, a towheaded boy who had appeared a year before looking for work and been hired on by Royer with no questions asked about his background, finally said, "Ann Royer from Mexico? Is she your niece?"

"I'm afraid so. Do you know her?"

A telltale flush burned his tan cheeks and he stammered, "Sure do. I worked for her daddy two years before I come up here. What you said don't sound at all like her. She was real nice."

Royer raised his brows high. "Oh? She isn't now. I wonder. The shock of finding her father and mother killed by bandits and the ranch burned could have hurt her mind, changed her, frozen her. She is on Twin R now, running me out."

The boy looked stricken sick and said nothing more. At the wagon the cook was filling plates, dealing them around as the hushed crew filed past the tailgate. Bo

109

Short stood up but did not reach for a plate. He went off alone, head down, kicking at rocks and sticks, too disturbed to eat.

Neither Pat nor Phil Royer wanted food either but Wallace insisted they must take it to sustain them through the long night ride. When they had choked down all they could the Royers shook hands around, Royer suggesting as he handed each his wages that they might stay on as a crew for Frank Pease. But not one of them would work for the old man.

It was dusk when the three lined out with the pack horse on a lead rope carrying the blanket rolls and a second grub bag from the wagon stores. By dawn they were far south, stopped for a breakfast, slept until the sun overhead waked them with its hot blaze, and took the trail again. They were days crossing the vast flats of west Texas before they reached the giant gorge at the edge of the Big Bend.

It was new territory to Dork Wallace, different from any he had known, a land of towering mountains that looked like crumpled brown paper bags, of deep canyons and flat topped mesas, deserts of greasewood, thorn bush, dagger and great fields of chino grass. But also there were long stretches of grazing land, the best ranch country he had ever seen. Most of these were lush with underground water although some had only tinajas, natural rock holes filled with water from a source perhaps a hundred miles away.

The deeper they went the more empty, lifeless the Bend seemed, more forbidding, giving rise to the sensation that the ghosts of Apaches, who had roasted

110

their sotol over fires ringed in stone circles, kept a jealous watch of their old haunts. Wallace was not superstitious but an air lay over everything that chilled him. There were no human habitations, no one anywhere within sight. Dork felt the brooding pressure on him strongly when they made camp beside a shallow, crystal stream. As dark came after their supper and they sat around the little eye of fire, night brought apprehension with it. He asked Royer, "Do you feel ghosts around here?"

The rancher nodded, building a cigarette. "I know what you mean. Everyone who comes in this country is conscious of an eeriness. I was introduced to it when Randal moved here just after the war and I helped him drive a herd through. Made me curious so I stayed three months, exploring. One place I found a whole community of caves with pictures drawn on the walls a long, long time ago. My cousin has a way with Apaches, has treaties with the chiefs that they've never broken. He had two herding for him and I asked them about the caves, if they knew who had lived there and what the pictures meant. They said, *the old ones*, and didn't know any more than that."

Wallace's own curiosity came alive about this vast empty area. When he asked, Royer told him that after the revolution that had overthrown Maximilian in Mexico and ruined cattle and mining in the northern part, there had been almost no new development in the Big Bend, and only a few widely scattered ranches surviving the raiding bandit gangs.

Continuing south their trail crossed the Rio Bravo, turned to follow its course downstream, and late in the day an arch of thick posts marked the entrance of a lane. A sign hung on chains with letters burned deep identified the Double R ranch. They rode under that and crossed a spreading pastureland of rich grass. A leisurely creek snaked through it out of a canyon still far ahead, a feeder stream of the Rio Grande some twenty miles south. It was a magnificent setting, the pasture lying in the arms of an imposing rock ridge over a thousand feet high, the headquarters built on a bench at the base of the cliffs with an overview of endless miles. Sleek, fat cattle grazed the meadow. A rail fence kept them out of the yard.

As they reached the gate a white-haired man with a military bearing came from the house, a rifle cradled across his left arm. In this lonely, forgotten land any visitor was automatically classed an enemy until he proved otherwise. The buildings here were fortresses of logs, the windows narrow slits, designed to withstand siege. Phil Royer sent a rebel yell across the yard before he led them to the porch. The man there threw both hands over his head, leaned the rifle against the railing, loped down the steps and out to meet the party, calling as he came up.

"Phil . . . You're a sight for sore eyes. And is that Pat, all grown up? What are you doing down here at roundup time?"

He pumped Phil's hand when he got down, reached up to lift the girl out of her saddle, held her against him for a hearty kiss, then gave Dork Wallace a quick appraisal. Phil made the introduction, then in short, bitter sentences told of the loss of Twin R.

Randal Royer heard him out, his frown deepening, then sighed. "So Howard and Martha are dead. Phil, I never saw him after the day I caught that Yankee bullet at Vicksburg. I never saw his daughter. How could they raise such a child?"

"Only explanation I can think of is that the murders deranged her. Well, there's no help for it. Can you put us up for a few weeks?"

"Long as you'll stay and glad to have you. I'm short handed. Got four Mexicans and five Indians but two others left me last week. Phil, if you've a mind to ranch around here I know a real good valley west about ten miles that will pasture as big a herd as mine and I'll stake you to enough cows to start you. Help you build as soon as there's time. Tomorrow I'll show you the place. It'll be good to have you close by."

They rode out in the early morning. Looking at the green gem Wallace's mouth watered. If there were other such places unclaimed, one day he could have his own ranch.

He played with that dream for three weeks while he helped with the roundup, then joined the drive to the railroad at Sanderson.

When the cattle were penned in the shipping yards Randal took him and Phil to the Mexican adobe cantina to wash the dust out of their throats. It was a busy room, the counter lined solid, but the bartender spotted Randal and beckoned him to wedge in, poured three glasses, and passed them across, saying, "Man

113

was in here a while ago asking how to find a family named Royer."

Handing glasses over his shoulder to his cousin and Wallace, Randal asked, "Know who he is?"

"Didn't say, but if he's still in town you'll likely find him at Ma Green's chili shack eating supper."

They tossed the drinks down and left, found the little restaurant and went in, stopping to adjust their eyes to the dimness after the bright sun of the street. As soon as he could see, Phil grunted his surprise and walked quickly to a table. The towhead Bo Short was there eating, but did not see them until Phil stopped beside him, saying, "Bo, was it you asking for a Royer place?"

The boy started, came around, and his face lighted. "Boss . . . yeah. I was about to give up looking for you. They said at the livery I'd have to have someone with me who knew the Big Bend if I was to find the Royer spread. I've been hunting you since the day after you left Twin R."

"What for?"

"I found out something you ought to know. You remember that last night just before you took off, I said I knew Ann Royer? Worked for her daddy? Well, I just couldn't believe she'd turned so mean. Next day I rode in to see for myself. She was mean all right, snapped my head off, told me I was fired for leaving the roundup. But she is not the Ann Royer I knew in Mexico. Don't even look like my Ann."

CHAPTER
ELEVEN

Phil Royer sank down on the chair opposite Bo Short so hard that one leg cracked, his eyes boring the boy, and fired his question like a shot.

"You're certain?"

"I ought to be. I've been saving up for three years to get a stake so I could ask her to marry me. If that was Ann I'd have got kissed as soon as I rode in."

"Do you know who the girl at Twin R is?"

"Never laid eyes on her."

The Royer cousins looked at each other blankly. Dork Wallace asked, "Did you call her? Tell her you know she's an impostor?"

"I sure didn't. I was knocked for a loop. Didn't say a word, just climbed on my horse and lit. First thing I thought of was to go to Mexico and see what was going on. Then it seemed Phil should hear as soon as I could find him."

Phil Royer blew out a gust of breath. "I'm damned glad you came. Now I don't know whether or not my brother is dead. I'll have to go down and see and find out who stole my ranch."

"That makes two of us," Bo Short said urgently. "I've got to know about Ann."

"Mind if I ride along?" Wallace wanted to know. "I'd like to see that country and you might want another hand."

Phil nodded. "I was going to ask you. Randal, I'll leave Pat with you."

But Patricia Royer had a very different idea when they trailed back to the Double R. She was not going to be left behind to worry through the weeks, and in the end she wore her father down. Randal Royer wanted to join them but could not leave while so much work must be done.

They took extra horses because Bo Short warned that the Sierras they must cross were more rugged than anything in Texas. Randal gave them directions for the first leg of the trip, following Regan Canyon where the ranch was, down to Shafter Crossing on the Rio Grande. Beyond that he did not know the way. Bo Short said he did. When they forded the river three trails converged. Theirs was westbound, through the Ladrones Mountains until they cut the road from El Paso south to Chihuahua City at the fringe of the Sierra Madre del Norte.

After the flats of Texas the range that split Mexico into east and west parts like a spine was an awesome challenge. The trail took them up through jumbled badlands to towering peaks separated by mile-deep canyons, through heavy timber and mammoth rocks. They found startling valleys nested below the bleak heights, fertile, lush with tangled growth of fruit trees once cultivated but now gone wild. Again they rode through clumps of giant pines, past thorn trees that

116

snagged their clothes, others with gnarled red bark looking as if they had been full grown when Columbus sailed to America.

In this ancient, timeless land the sense that a thousand eyes watched them was much stronger to Dork Wallace than it had been on the Big Bend, but in all the days of crossing they saw no human being. The girl felt it too, riding close at Wallace's side wherever the trail allowed, her eyes searching for hidden lookouts behind rocks and trees.

They wound down a narrow canyon with almost vertical walls to a bottom that widened to a valley ten miles across. The canyon stream snaked through deep, thick grass as green as emerald and cattle, but very few, grazed along the banks. Halfway across the big pasture a blackened stone chimney rose like an obelisk in the middle of charred timbers that had once been a large house. Other charred piles identified where the outbuildings had stood. All had been burned not long ago since no grass had begun encroaching on the ashes.

Here was the reality of all the Sierra boded, destruction and death.

Bo Short reined in, and when the others came abreast said in a flat, controlled voice, "This is where your brother lived, Phil. Where I knew Ann. Damn them."

Reluctantly he put the horse forward, walked it slowly around the site of the house but could not bring himself to do what must be done. Dork Wallace understood. He dismounted, went to the pack horse for the shovel and systematically dug through the ash

117

looking for burned bones. The grisly search turned nothing up either here or in the outbuilding rubble. It was late in the day when he finished and walked upstream to where the others had made a camp, were sitting silent, staring unseeing into a small fire.

Dork stopped beside Royer. "No sign of anybody being in there. They could have been away. They may be all right."

Phil's head barely moved, sideways. "No. If they were they'd have come to me."

"Do you know of any friends they had down here?"

The man thought for minutes, then drew a deep sigh. "I know a name. When he'd been here a year Howard wrote about a French priest, Father Louis in Chihuahua City, who had helped him get acquainted. But neither Pat nor I speak Spanish. Do you?"

"I know Cholo," Short told them. "We can locate him through the church or the *jefe* . . . the police chief."

In the morning they climbed again, went back to the capital town across the range and were directed by the *alcalde* to the parish house behind the small adobe cathedral. A squat Indian woman answered the knock and took Royer's name to the priest. Father Louis hurried through the dim, cool corridor, the bottom of his habit flapping around his short legs, greeting them in heavily accented English, then led the party back to his study.

There, switching between English and Spanish with Bo Short translating, the *padre* said he had been expecting Royer for some weeks after his brother's death. No, the raiders had not been found but they were known to be Pedro Rojas' men. He asked if they wanted to see the graves.

Astonished, Phil Royer said, "They're buried here?"

They were. A *mozo* of Howard's crew had been cutting wood in the mountains the day of the attack, had seen the smoke and gone to the edge of timber to find out what it was. Howard's riders were all out finishing the roundup, the family was alone. Rojas had dragged them into the yard, shot them, then driven off the half of the herd that was already gathered there. After the bandits were gone the *mozo* took the wood wagon down, laid the bodies in it, and brought them to the church.

Father Louis took them to the graveyard where three fresh headstones were carved Howard, Martha, and Ann Royer. Bo Short stood at the foot of the girl's mound, his hands clenching in spasms, the fingers curling as if folding around his guns, his eyes stretched wide to keep moisture back.

At length the padre broke the long silence, a deep concern in his soft voice. "If you did not know they had been brought here it must be that Lida did not reach you. Because she is American and speaks English well I sent her with the *mozo* as escort to take you the sad word. Now I fear for her."

Phil Royer's mind snapped back from the past he had been recalling. "What's that? Lida who?"

"Lida Grant, an orphan raised at the convent. Ann went to their school and the girls were close friends. If harm has come to her I must forever blame myself."

119

"None has . . . yet." Royer's tone was bleak. "A blond girl appeared in Del Rio representing herself as Ann Royer. Since I had never seen my niece I believed her. But she's a poor friend. She knew my ranch had originally been my brother's and is still carried in his name and she claimed to have inherited it. Married an old range robber and together they drove us off."

The priest sighed, nodding slowly. "Yes. Lida is capable of that. She was a wily child, not to be trusted, though Ann defended her because she had no parents. I should not have relied on her. I am sorry."

"Never mind. I appreciate the intent, and I can take the ranch back if you will write a certification that Ann Royer is dead."

"Indeed I will, and you should also ask the *jefe* for a copy of his record."

Back in the study Phil Royer waited while Father Louis wrote and signed the paper, then went on to the street where the others waited in the bright, hot sunlight. They visited the *jefe*, then with the proof in his pocket he stood debating, made a decision, and said, "So Rojas got only half Howard's herd and the rest must still be around the ranch. Before we go home it ought to be worth while to round them up, bring them here, and sell them. Pat, you can wait in town for us."

She gave him a cloying smile. "I can ride too, and the more hands we have the sooner we can comb them out of the brush, the sooner we can go tell Frank Pease he married a ringer. Let's go."

CHAPTER
TWELVE

Marriage to Frank Pease was much more an ordeal than anything Lida Grant thought she had bargained for. In the few days she had known him she had recognized his meanness, his greed, but she had not seen how vindictive he could be.

Finding that her gun had been stolen was her first rude shock when he moved her to the Lazy P. Because she had shut him out on their wedding night he made a slavey of her at the ranch, fired the Chinese cook, demanded that she feed the crew, wash their clothes, and keep the unbelievably cluttered two-room cabin. His method of coercion was her next comeuppance. When she balked he tied her to the corral fence and left her until she surrendered, with the threat of firing any man who let her loose.

Rather than living as the owner of Twin R the girl was a captive on her husband's land suffering such drudgery and indignities as she had never known with the sisters of the convent. But at least Pease left her alone for two weeks.

Then came a Saturday when the crew rode to Del Rio immediately after breakfast. Pease did not go with them. Lida was in the cookshack, up to her elbows in soapy, greasy dishwater trying for the thousandth time to think of an escape that would not cost her Twin R. She had already considered divorcing the husband she had and marrying Spangler Cooper instead, but discarded the idea. Frank Pease would surely kill any other man she turned to. Hating him, she took out her frustration in banging pots and pans, slamming the tin plates in a racket of fury.

She heard the door open but ignored the sound. A moment later Pease was beside her, his claw around one arm, his voice rough.

"Time now you act like a wife, you little minx. Right now, and we got the whole day by ourselves."

Her reaction was an instinctive jump away, picking up the dishpan, throwing pan and water at his head. The lip of the pan cut his face. He stood dripping grease and blood while she ran, dodging around the big work table, putting it between them. Pease's shriek was ear splitting.

"Why damn you. I'll take a buggy whip to you for that."

She yelled back, exploding. "If I had a gun I'd shoot you dead. I'd love to see you dead. I'd have this whole end of Texas and I'd sell it all and go to Paris and live like a lady instead of a slave."

He had grabbed up the dish towel, mopping at his eyes, starting after her, then stopped short. A slow, hungry grin wiped the rage off his mouth and he laughed.

"You'd sell out, would you? Well hell, girlee, why didn't you say that to start with? I'll buy Twin R right now. Give you five thousand dollars for it. That's what the stock is worth. As to land, you only own the one section where the buildings are, the rest is government range open to anybody . . ."

Lida Grant did not know what the ranch was really worth but she felt certain it was much more than Frank Pease's offer. It was the rancher's nature to cheat as much as he could. Still, here was her chance to be free of him. She swallowed hard.

"I'll sell for ten."

"All right, ten. It's worth it to be rid of you for good. Now clean up this mess while I go saddle and we'll go have Spang Cooper make up the papers today before I change my mind. Ten thousand's a heap of money."

The girl hurried, her breath coming in small gasps as she finished the kitchen and ran to put on the only dress Frank had bought for her. He had two horses waiting below the porch when she came out and in an unusual show of gallantry helped her to the saddle. Frank pushed the pace so that they were in Del Rio by midafternoon.

Saturday was Spangler Cooper's busiest day, when all the ranchers and crews of the area normally came in. He was at his office window when the Peases tied up at the hitch rail directly below and climbed the stairs. Accustomed to the rancher visiting him every time he came to town, he had not expected the old man to bring his young wife to overhear whatever business he was here to talk about, but he was pleased at the chance to press his acquaintance, bowing over her hand, complimenting her costume. Then he all but fell on his face at Pease's first words.

"Spang, cut out the play acting and make us up a deed for Annie to sign. She's selling me Twin R."

The lawyer straightened, searching the girl's face, trying for words twice before he managed, "Why in the world would you do that?"

She said sharply, "I can't stand living here so I'm going to Europe."

Cooper sank weakly into his chair, seeing his hope of having the ranch himself fly out of the window. Keeping his face empty he fumbled through drawers, brought up a form for a quitclaim deed, laid it before him, and asked, "How much is Ace paying you for the property?"

"Ten thousand."

Pease cut in, "For the cows and water and one section. That's all she owns."

In spite of his cold control the lawyer blurted, "Ten thousand? . . . Why . . ."

Pease's yelp cut him short. "That's what she asked and if you want to stay my lawyer you write it up that way."

Cooper looked from one to the other for a long moment. It was on the tip of his tongue to offer the girl twice that price, still far short of the ranch's real worth, but caution stopped him. That would make Frank Pease his mortal enemy. He could win a court case against the rancher but he knew the vicious old robber would never let a fight reach a courtroom. He felt as if he had Twin R in his hand and it was running through his fingers like dry sand. Flexing them to put away the illusion he reached for a quill and began to write. When the paper was finished he turned it for Ann to sign, added his signature as witness, and shoved it toward Pease. It was all he could do to keep his voice steady.

"Take it to the courthouse and have it recorded. Good-by."

Back on the street Frank Pease sounded more considerate than the girl had ever heard him. "Now we'll stop at the bank, get you a letter of credit that you can take with you."

She stopped him on the slatted sidewalk. After Cooper's reaction she knew she was being badly cheated and she did not know whether Pease could pull some other trick to make a letter of credit worthless after she had left. In a flat, determined voice she said, "I want the money in cash."

Pease looked aghast with genuine concern. "You what? You can't carry ten thousand dollars around in cash. You'll have it stolen. I'll open an account for you and you can write checks."

"Cash, Frank. And a gun."

A grudging admiration twisted his thin lips. "Well, you've got by this far on your own. Maybe you can get away with it."

At the bank Hyde Stewart hid his curiosity when Frank Pease withdrew ten thousand in cash and handed it to his wife, watched her tuck the bills in the bottom of her handbag and clasp that close under her arm. It was his practice never to ask questions of the rancher and open himself to one of the famous rages, but when they had gone he followed them to the door, watched them go into the courthouse, and made his guess. The girl from Mexico could be counted as the rancher's latest victim.

With the deed recorded Pease became the gallant, took his wife for an early supper at the hotel, bought her a second dress and a traveling case, a ticket on the San Antonio stage, and a small gun for her bag, but did not give that to her until the coach lumbered in and he handed her up to a seat. The last thing he did for her, as the driver took the team out was toss a box of shells through the window. She would not have time to load and try to shoot him before she was out of range. And it was sharp in his mind that as his widow she would inherit an empire. Not until the stage was out of sight and he was sure she was gone did he begin to hunt for the Chinese cook.

Lida Grant Pease sank heavily against the seat back, her hands hidden in her deep handbag loading the new gun. She had not gotten full value for the ranch, but then it had not been her ranch in the first place, and ten thousand was more money than she had ever seen. She had intended packing it in the traveling case, but Pease had insisted on carrying that, loading it in the boot, when it would have been easy for him to lift the packet out. As it was she was sure of it and could move it at the first stop.

Through the years at school she had been jealous of Ann Royer who had everything, including a family, while she had nothing. Then the news of the Rojas murders had come like a bombshell. Ann had trusted Lida as her confidant, had told her the whole history of

126

her people, and the idea flamed up that if she could make her way to Texas she could pose as the niece Phil Royer had never seen, could claim the ranch. She had had no money for the trip but she had convinced Father Louis that as Ann's closest friend she should be sent north to break the news.

It had been pure luck after she turned her escort back at the river that she had found the Lazy P. She could have lived at Twin R, but with Phil Royer in control she could never have sold it. Frank Pease had made that possible. Now in so short a time she was on her way into the world, a thick sheaf of money warm in her lap, under the weight of the gun that would protect it.

Until now she had not been on a stage. She had not been out of Chihuahua except for two visits with Ann Royer to their ranch, and she was wary of the other passengers, using a trick she had developed in school of watching her classmates and the nuns without being caught at it.

There were four men, two dressed as cowboys who had slung saddles on top of the coach before they climbed inside, another man dressed in black, a flat crown, wide brim hat pulled over his eyes, a knee length coat over a white shirt with a ruffled breast, and a diamond stickpin in a black tie. Beside her a fat man with a derby wheezed through a pouting mouth and fastened prominent brown eyes on her. Quickly she dropped hers and drew away against the coach wall.

The miles fell behind, flat, monotonous land that hypnotized her to drowsiness as it wheeled past.

127

Combined with the vehicle swaying like a cradle she found herself dozing as night came down. The men now napped, heads sunk on their chests, but she dared not sleep for fear that her bag might be taken. She fought against it, was sure that she had not closed her eyes until a grating voice, loud through the window, startled her into jumping.

"Louden's station. We lay over to daylight. Grub in the dining room."

The driver was at the door, pulling it open. The stage was stopped before a small hotel, the passengers rousing, getting stiffly to the ground. The man in black, opposite Lida, swung out, turned and offered her a hand down the step and when she stood beside him tucked her fingers under his elbow.

"May I? The footing is rough in the poor light."

She tensed but let him pilot her across the deep furrows of the 'dobe yard and into the little lobby. The pendulum clock on the wall above the desk read midnight. So she had slept. But she felt more tired than when she had gotten aboard the stage.

The stranger turned her toward the arch and the dining room but she pulled away, saying, "I'm not hungry. I just want to lie down."

The thought had flashed that while she and the other passengers slept this man could have searched her bag. The bulk and weight of the money and gun were still there, but he would not have risked taking them, having them found on him in the confined coach if she missed them and cried theft. He reminded her of Spangler Cooper, wily, trying to strike an acquaintance that

128

could put him alone with her somewhere along the road. Yet he did not insist, only lifted his hat and went on to the tables. But suspicion that she was watched kept her from asking for her case from the boot.

Lida swung back to the desk, paid the bald clerk there a dollar for a room and climbed to the upper floor. The key he gave her turned around and around in the lock. The cramped cubicle beyond the door was stifling with stale, foul-smelling air that barely stirred when she got the single window unstuck and raised. She lit the lamp, saw walls hung with flour sacks, the brand names stamped on them, a thin, lumpy mattress on a sagging bed. Since the lock on the door was broken she pulled the head of the bedframe against it, took off only her shoes and lay down, slipped the bag under her skirt as high as her waist, and kept the gun in her hand beneath the pillow.

Again she was waked, by a hammering on the door and a yell in the corridor.

"Daylight. Stage leaves in fifteen minutes."

Groggy, the girl crossed the spur-splintered floor, dabbed tepid, dust-coated water from the pitcher against her face, got into her shoes and went down for a hurried breakfast. With the others she wolfed steak and beans, swallowed half a cup of coffee, then was first into the coach. The cowboys and the fat man came aboard but the stranger in black did not appear. The driver came with the mail sack over his shoulder, climbed to the high seat, the hostler stepped back from the horses' heads and at a high yell and a snap of the long whip the team lurched into a loping run, the wheels bumping out of the rutted yard to the main trail. Still Lida had not had a chance to transfer the money.

The fat man had moved across to the seat beside her, filling space enough for two, his knees spread apart as though to brace himself against the bounce and sway. But every time the coach tipped his thigh swung against hers, his shoulder bumped her arm. Lida shrank to the wall but he was soon crowding her again until she said, "Please . . . you'll push me out."

He turned his head, the full red mouth rounding in pretended surprise, the bold eyes shoved close to her face, and a chuckle rumbled from him.

"Kind of a rough ride ain't it, cutie? We just got to make the best of it in this godforsaken blast furnace, take it with a smile. You got a real friendly smile I'll bet. Say, I got my sample case right here. A little nip or two'll help while the miles away."

Lida raised her chin high, looked out of the window. The fat man spread a thick palm on her leg.

"Hey, you got no call to be sore, we . . ."

His words cut off short. The cowboy opposite him had moved fast, stretching his boot forward to draw his gun with one hand, then leaning, reaching his other to pinch and twist the thick-lobed ear, haul the fat man sideways away from the blond girl while he hammered the gun snout on the coach roof, calling to the driver.

"Haul up, Jink. Man in here wants to ride on top with you."

The fat man squealed like a pig at the sudden pain. "Lemme go, damnit. I like it right here."

The cowboy kept twisting the ear as the team slowed. "On top or walk. Take your choice."

The second cowboy, against the far door, shoved it open, jerking his head at it when the coach stopped, but said nothing. His partner lowered the gun, leveled it on the big belly, let the ear go, and the point was made. Muttering under his breath the drummer picked up his case, got out and climbed clumsily onto the roof. The door was pulled closed, the stage rolled on, the pair inside not so much as glancing at each other.

Lida said quietly, "Thank you," her eyes down on the hands folded over her bag.

"Ma'am, it was a pleasure."

The girl did not see the flush climb the tanned cheeks. She was being torn two ways. She was afraid of a possibly developing conversation, of questions asked that she would have to invent answers to, but also there was a growing aloneness, suspicion isolating her when what she wanted was to enjoy a companionship. She thought of Dork Wallace and hated him for resisting her. With him she could have been happy, wealthy, powerful. There would have been no need for this fear of everyone who spoke to her.

The two men talked together idly, laughing over private jokes hinted at but not explained, shutting her out. She watched the endless plain, the breaks where cottonwood clumps marked water holes and streams, endured the blazing heat that would increase as the hours ran on.

Then, still short of the noon stop by fifteen miles the stage was yanked to a jarring stop where the road crossed a bridge between trees on either side. Two masked men appeared, one at each window, guns aimed at both cowboys. She knew there would be others holding the driver and the fat man. The pair were there, looking in, before she had time to think of hiding the bag that lay in plain sight on her knees. The voice of the man on her side came muffled through his handkerchief.

"Reach across careful, honey. Don't get in my sights. Take the boys' guns one at a time and toss them out here, and don't count on me not to shoot you if you try a trick. You two, lift your hands up on your shoulders."

The cowboy who had run the fat man off smiled a reassurance, said in an easy tone, "Do just like he says, ma'am. We lose a little money it ain't important as keeping a whole skin."

He raised his arms, twisted his hip to make it easier for her to reach his holster. The blond girl bent forward, took the gun butt with her thumb and forefinger, drew it, and at arm's length swung it slowly out of the window and dropped it. She had to hunch along the seat to reach the second gun and let it fall from the other window, then sat rigid, looking from one road agent to the other, deliberately folding her full skirt over her bag and right hand with her left.

The bandit spoke again. "You cowpokes, open that door yonder, climb out, and stand quiet to one side unless you want the lady hurt."

The masked man on the far side backed away, covering them as they got awkwardly to the ground and moved away from the door.

"Now you, honey," the order came.

Lida stood up, bent almost double to avoid the roof, backed to the side of the coach, lowered one foot to the step, then the other to the ground, From that position she shot away the face at the opposite window, spun, and before he could bring his gun around from the cowboys, fired into the chest of the man just behind her.

As he stumbled back and fell both cowboys jumped, one for his own gun, the other for the one the bandit dropped, intentionally knocking the girl off her feet. Neither had reached the weapons when three explosions cracked almost as one from the head of the team. The two boys dived on, face down in the grit of the road, not moving again.

Lida in falling instinctively threw her arms wide. The open bag flew out of her hand, spilling the packet of money. Her finger spasmed on her trigger but the bullet went into the ground. She had one brief, blurred glimpse of a man dressed in black, a white shirt below a mask before his third shot slammed into her, killed her as her back landed on the dirt.

While he walked to her body and bent to pick up ten thousand dollars a fourth man held a shotgun on the driver and fat man atop the stage. The killer rifled the still figures, took the gold ring from the girl's finger, watches and small amounts of cash from the cowboys and the dead outlaw, tossed their guns over the side of the bridge, then went around the coach for whatever of value was on the other man of his party.

Back at the head of the team he beckoned the two on the high seat down, knocked both unconscious with his muzzle and went through their pockets. Last, he searched through the baggage in the boot, used Lida's new traveling case to carry the loot, took the liquor salesman's sample case under the arm that held the valise, walked back toward the robber who guarded the unconscious driver and guard and when he was too close for a possible miss shot the man through the heart.

He and the horses they had ridden were far away when the driver and fat man came to.

The team and stage were gone, bolted he supposed, but with a fifteen mile walk ahead in the broiling sun Jink Jones, twenty years a driver who had never lost a passenger in a holdup before, counted himself miraculously lucky to be alive this hour. Jink stood up, wobbly on his legs to begin with, turned a slow circle surveying the massacre. Three of the four road agents lay widely scattered and that gave him a grim satisfaction. But the two cowboys had been his friends, frequent passengers on his stage. Those he regretted, puzzled by their positions, face down, hands stretched toward guns they must have dropped in falling. He wondered at their foolhardiness in having drawn against the two bandits near them, when they surely had known there were others. In a mistaken effort to protect the blond girl? She had been an eye catcher all right. Poor little bride whom old Frank Pease had unaccountably managed to snare into marriage, bound, he supposed for a shopping spree in San Anton. It occurred to Jink that Frank might melt enough to pay a man who brought her remains home for burial.

134

Walking to where she lay Jink picked up the handbag, was startled to see two holes rimmed with powder burns in it, and the little gun still beside her hand. So it had been she who had panicked and exploded the shootout. Women and guns, they never mixed. Sighing, he dropped the weapon in his pocket, stuffed the handbag on top of it, and hoisted the limp body over his shoulder.

Well into the afternoon he carried Lida, the fat man puffing beside him, toward the station they should have made by dinner time. Somewhat short of it the stage appeared, driven toward him with a posse coming to find why it had pulled in with nobody aboard. Jink told a reenactment of the holdup, describing the only bandit who had survived, as the team was turned and they were taken to the station. There Jones rented a light rig and two horses, loaded the dead girl in it, and drove straight through to the Lazy P, racing the temperature that was beginning to affect the corpse.

Frank Pease showed little appreciation, ordered an immediate burial, flew into a rage that the money was lost, and sent Jink Jones away without so much as a meal. Then with his own brand of humor the rancher rewarded his bride and firmed his claim to Twin R with a headboard set over the grave behind the corral, out of sight, carved to read:

ANN ROYER PEASE. BELOVED WIFE OF FRANK PEASE.
R.I.P.

CHAPTER
THIRTEEN

In Mexico Dork Wallace, Royer, and Short spent five days in the brush on the western slope of the shallow canyon hazing cows down to the lush grass along the stream near where the trail entered the valley. Patricia picked them up in small snaggles, herding them into a loose group that could be kept together by occasionally circling it. With so few working it would be impossible to comb the distant eastern wall and the canyon steepened too sharply on the south to make that area at all productive. By the fifth evening some two hundred animals were gathered, about as many as they could push across the mountain trail at one time.

The shadows were deep on the valley floor when Wallace built the small fire and went to the creek for water. Turning back to the camp something took his eyes up, some movement, something different above them. There was still sunlight, blue sky on the canyon rim. Silhouetted against the blue a line of riders sat. He counted ten. Cone-shaped figures in ponchos topped with tall, wide brimmed hats. Mexicans certainly. Raiders probably. And the little herd made a tempting darker mass against the grass for them to look down on. He strode back to the fire, pointing.

136

"Too many to stand off. Get into the timber. Bo, is there another way out of here that we can reach in the dark?"

An animal growl came from the towhead. "Only way across the basin. You're better off to ride part way up here and lay low the night. I'm going to stay close. If they come down now I want a crack at them when they go to sleep."

"No." Phil Royer was looking at his daughter, his expression saying that if she were not here the three men could try Short's way. "We stay together. Wait until they take the cows up, then follow them. We can pick off those that ride drag along the way."

They saddled. By the time they were mounted the dark was deep enough to hide the direction they took, angling up the slope away from the trail into the dense timber midway up. There they tied the horses and sat quiet. Shortly the jangle of harness came down, passed them, continued to the camp they had left, the fire that still burned. That was built higher. Black figures moving in front of it made a blinking light. A draft sucked up the wall brought odors of smoke and food cooking to remind them they had not eaten since noon. Afterward a guitar was played, heavy laughter and singing suggested tequila or pulque. Finally, toward midnight it was quiet below. A moon rose, filtering light through the treetops.

Dork Wallace said, "Let's move away from the horses and catch some sleep."

They found places at a distance where if some night hunting cat should attack the animals the people would

137

not be prey, but Wallace stayed close enough to get back and stop a marauder. The dark hours passed without disturbance. When Dork roused the moon was gone, the sky was paling but it was still night beneath the trees. The light came slowly, showing him first the horses standing hipshot, heads down, not stirring. Then one lifted its muzzle and wickered softly. From the corner of his eye Dork caught movement downgrade, rolled, and had his gun trained on the place by the time he made out a figure climbing. He held his fire, drawing his hunting knife with his left hand to take the fellow with the blade if he could so that a shot would not bring others.

It was not a Mexican who appeared, but Bo Short. Grim satisfaction made a white line around his tight mouth. With a sinking premonition Dork Wallace slammed his question.

"Where have you been?"

"Below. I got one of the bastards, sliced his throat. He was standing guard in the moonlight. I couldn't locate the others, they're someplace in the dark."

Wallace cursed him. "You damned fool, now they'll know we didn't just hi-tail when we spotted them. They'll be on watch and we'll have less chance of taking them on the trail."

Short said drily, "You better take the Royers on out now. I want Rojas' scalp for Ann. I'll hang around."

Phil Royer had waked and overheard and agreed with Short. "I want Rojas for Martha and Howard too. We're not running but we're not separating either. We follow as we planned, but we'll have to be more careful."

Dork Wallace grunted. He might be Royer's foreman in name but what did that mean if he wasn't obeyed? Reason told him he should take the rancher and his daughter across the mountains ahead of the herd, abandon the little scrub bunch to the bandits, see Pat to safety, but no one listened.

"At least," he said, "get up over the rim, into the hills until they pass. Wait here and we'll be sitting ducks crossing that bare shelf."

Royer admitted that was true. They roused the girl, wound up the trail, rode across the exposed rim before sunrise. Looking down Wallace saw no movement, only small mounds wrapped in bright serapes still sleeping.

On top the mountains ran east in a ragged jumble of rock outbursts and rising canyons thick with timber where Wallace chose a vantage point. Hidden in the trees they could see the herd when it passed below them, and if they were discovered a retreat was open up the maze of intersecting draws. There they waited until noon, when a yipping of voices told that the cattle were being driven up the trail. In time the animals appeared, two riders at the head to keep them from straying into the brush, three others on either side along the column that twisted through the hills, and a ninth riding drag.

Wallace let out his held breath. There had been ten last night. Bo Short had killed one, and the rest were accounted for here. Short wanted to trail them immediately, to take out the last man at the nearest turn where he was not in sight of those ahead, put the serape and conical hat on Pat to take his place, and watch for the next chance for Wallace and himself to jump the next pair. Dork and Phil Royer would replace them while Bo went ahead for another. In that way, he thought, they could whittle down the odds without discovery. Then in some meadow, stampede the cows and in the melee wipe out the remainder.

Wallace argued to lie back, wait for night, go in on a sleeping camp when they could knife them all at once. Pedro Rojas had terrorized the border country for too long and Dork had no compunction at taking this advantage in view of the opportunity and the unequal numbers. But even Pat Royer voted against him this time, wanting to play a role herself. For the first time he saw virtue in the Texas law that forbade women a decision.

When the herd was half a mile beyond them they lined down to the trail, Bo Short in the lead and Wallace somewhat behind him. Phil Royer was to keep his daughter well back until Bo, if he succeeded, had dispatched his Mexican. They had the help of a gritty dust cloud to screen them, undulating around the turns. Gaining on the slow-moving cattle Dork Wallace saw Bo Short disappear into the cloud. He heard no sound, no warning shout. When the dust subsided there the towhead was on the ground, the Mexican on top of him but rolling off, blood flowing from his throat. Short stripped the bright cloth over the head before it was too stained, raised it and the hat high to signal for Pat.

She was brought forward, mounted on the Mexican paint horse, and as she pushed on against the rear animals she could easily pass as the original rider.

The three men rode ahead, easing toward the nearest outriders, keeping low in the saddles among the bawling cattle until the two tall hats loomed out of the roiling dust. Bo Short took the one on the right, Dork Wallace the left with Phil Royer close behind Short. Again the riders were hit without warning and knifed. The bandit band was cut to six.

Wallace and Short in serapes and hats pressed on, upright, playing the part of herders while Royer brought their horses. Then the herd slowed, all but stopped, and there were shouts ahead urging it on. The swale they were crossing narrowed, squeezed the trail into a defile between sheer walls that grew higher as they advanced. Only two cows and the two horsemen could ride abreast. Wallace remembered the place from the way in, a spiny ridge that divided two bowls about two acres each. And here could lay disaster.

It came when they were in the middle of the pass. A shot from the rocks above that hit Bo Short square, lifted him, hurled him flying out of the saddle. A second shot on the heels of the first spun Wallace's high hat away.

He shouted at Royer to drop off the horse. Both men did, crowding in among the cows that forced the mounts on through the slot. Bending low, beneath the curve of the fat bellies, turning to face the oncoming animals, they gave ground, backing with the pack, barely able to keep their feet. If they did not, if they fell,

141

the hoofs would trample them to pulp. Grabbing one long horn in both hands Dork Wallace let the brute drag him, kicking with his boots to stay between the front legs. For a hundred feet he was carried that way, not knowing what had become of the rancher.

Then he was through the narrow gate. The animal swerved aside as the trail widened. He heard raucous laughter. A hand appeared in front of his face holding a gun. It clouted the steer across the nose. Another hand took hold of his collar and yanked him out of the path of the lumbering pack, held him up and the gun was jammed against his back.

The herd pushed past, spreading out in the bowl. The last of them came through. Opposite him he saw through the dust that two Mexicans had Phil Royer between them, on his feet but bent, both hands clenching one leg above the knee.

Worst of all, behind the dust cloud came the paint horse. Pat Royer was astride but no longer in the saddle. She sat on the withers, the hat gone, the serape torn down around her lap, her ash hair falling long across her shoulders. In the leather behind her a thick Mexican was solidly seated, one big arm around her waist, the other hand holding a wicked blade against her throat. A grin stretched his moon face wider than it was long.

"*He . . . aqui* . . . .Compadres, see the little chicken that flew into the coop." The English was fair, used for the benefit of the Americans.

Wallace stifled his groan. The lack of weight at his belt told him his gun had dropped somewhere in the pass, but it would have been of no use anyway. Patricia Royer would have been dead before he could draw. She looked at him and found a wry smile and shrug. More than anything she could have done that small gesture tore at his heart and he knew in a flash how important to him she had become.

He heard a scrambling in the rocks above and shortly the last two of the bandits dropped to the trail, those who had sat on top and fired on him and Bo Short. They came around into view, rifles trained on Wallace and Royer. The man on the horse threw rapid Spanish at them and the pair behind the captives, let go the girl's waist, grabbed her wrist, and twisted until she must fall or have her arm broken. He kept hold of her as she dropped, then stepped down beside her with a swagger.

"I am Pedro Rojas." It was a boast. "Pedro the Terrible. I do many bad things." On the word bad he jutted his chin forward, bared his big yellow teeth and waggled his head fast, then laughed. "I do many smart things too. Did you think when my guard was" — he slashed a finger across his throat — "I would not know you had not run away? Did you think I do not know every rock and bush and trail in the Sierra? So I ride past your hiding place like I am asleep. And I set the trap here in this good place. And I catch a big prize I think."

They were going to be killed. Wallace had no slightest doubt of that, knowing Rojas' reputation for brutality. The only questions were when and how, and since they had not already been shot Dork foresaw the Mexican playing cruel games until death released them. The only choice he had was to make Rojas mad enough to get it over with quickly. He made a sneering face.

"You're so smart you lost four men. That really takes brains."

The bandit wasn't even ruffled, only shrugged. "Life is cheap, señor. We all die one day. I have many more men when I want them. All want to ride with Pedro Rojas. Now let us talk business. This is your woman?"

"No."

"Then she belongs to the other whose leg hurts him, the rich gringo."

Wallace scoffed. "Everything he owns is on him. He had a ranch in Texas but it was stolen from him. He came here to gather what were left of his brother's cattle, these that you grabbed. Rojas, you're a two-bit piker beside the little witch who drove him off his place. You're a cheap bungler."

The man only grinned wider. "You make the foolish story. A woman does not take a ranch from a man. The man takes. I keep this pretty little hen with me and tomorrow I send her man and you to Chihuahua City to bring me a fat ransom. Fifty thousand pesos . . . a hundred thousand . . . I will think how much when I see what she is worth."

Phil Royer had straightened with Wallace's first words, horror in his eyes. That changed to bafflement as the talk went back and forth, to comprehension, and now seeing Dork's quick frown and slight headshake he bent over his leg again as if that were his greatest concern. He did not see Rojas' shove that sent the girl stumbling toward him. She fell, jarring against the knee that had been wrenched as he struggled among the cattle. He swore aloud, limped away, the man with the rifle moving with him. Neither Royer nor Dork Wallace made a move to help her.

Rojas giggled. "You think you fool me? Never mind, I have patience, I will wait."

In a sudden bellow he threw an order in Spanish at his band. Two of them ran for their horses, brought rawhide laces and tied the captives' hands behind their backs, lashed their legs together, the girl between the men. They could walk but only in concert.

Leaving them where they were the bandits moved down the trail, built a fire and made a meal. They did not feed the prisoners except for a little water. Afterward they brought the Royers' and Wallace's horses, untied their legs, and mounted them, stringing a lead line between them and Rojas' big animal. At the head of the herd they were towed through the afternoon. Near dusk the cows were scattered across a narrow valley where there was graze and a stream, the horses were picketed and an evening fire built.

Since Rojas' talk of a ransom Wallace had quit trying to bait the bandit. If they were not to be killed today or tonight there might be hope. But even if he and Royer were somehow able to come up with a fortune for the girl Dork knew none of them would be left alive after it was delivered. Honor was not Rojas' way. Whatever chance they had they would have to make for themselves before they were separated.

Then his hope faded and fear for Pat Royer ate into Wallace. He and Phil Royer were tied on opposite sides of a cottonwood near the stream. Rojas took the girl with him to the fire a hundred feet away, pushed her down to the grass and dropped cross-legged beside her. While a supper was cooked a skin of liquor passed around. Rojas drank deeply then yanked the girl's head back by the hair and poured into her throat. Both Wallace and Royer could see as he put the skin aside, dragged her against him, and ground his mouth against hers.

"Damn him." The words grated through her father's clenched teeth. "I'll rob a bank. I'll bring anything he says. God . . . don't let him hurt her."

"Be quiet," Wallace told him. "Keep your head. Look."

Pat Royer did not fight. She accepted the kiss and when Rojas drew back she laughed, then spoke at length. They could not tell what she said but the bandit listened, looked toward the tree, cocked his head on one side, and apparently questioned her. They talked further. Rojas shrugged, kissed her again, fed her more liquor, and took more himself. He did not handle her beyond that, until after they had eaten. Then as the guitar came out he pulled her to her feet and danced her around the circle. Others reached for her but Rojas flung them away. Drinking and dancing kept on until the moon overhead signaled midnight. One by one the five outlaws rolled in the serapes and slept. Rojas was the last to give up. Pat's hands were still tied at her back, now he tied her ankles, gestured her to lie down, pulled the serape off the nearest man and dropped it over her. He kneeled, kissed her once more, lay down close to her, and did not move.

Neither Royer nor Wallace slept. They worked at the rawhide until their wrists bled. It stretched, but not enough, and if the blood wet it enough it would shrink even tighter. The way they were tied they could not move to help each other, could not reach the thongs with their teeth.

The moon was well down and they had made no headway, had even lost as their sweat tightened the leather strings. Then they saw movement. Only a little, very slow. In the dim light they could not see what it was. After an interminable time one shadow separated itself from the other larger bulk. Gradually the space between them grew, Pat Royer inching away from Pedro Rojas. Then the movement was faster. She came rolling toward the tree, throwing herself from back to face. Wallace could hear Phil Royer's breath whistle through his teeth.

She reached them, sat up, hunched her back against the bole, and worked up it. Wallace felt the thong that bound his right wrist to Royer's left tugged. The girl rocked out and in. Abruptly the rawhide parted. Pat twisted her back toward Wallace. A shaft of moonlight winked off steel. She had a knife. Numb as his fingers were Dork Wallace worked them, took extraordinary care in finding the haft in her hand, in being sure of his hold before he took it from her. He cut his other arm loose, freeing Royer, slashed the binding around Pat's ankles, then that that held her wrists. She whispered.

"He's on his side, his holster on top. I didn't dare try for the gun but it's there."

Reaction to the long torment, the fruitless fight against the thongs, brought action without thought. Wallace wrapped her in his arms, tightened them, found her lips, and held them hard for a long moment. Phil Royer clamped a hand on his shoulder, pulled him back and took his place.

Wallace spun away, took the blade in his teeth to flex both hands as he ran, silent on the deep grass. Pedro Rojas' snores were loud, long, until the knife stopped them, slicing through the windpipe. Royer arrived as Dork lifted the gun and passed that to him, then used the knife once more. The rancher fired four times, one shot into each of the last four bandits. The first explosion waked them but none had time to raise up higher than one elbow before they were knocked back.

The little valley racketed with echoes. The cattle threw up their heads, bawled, milled, and broke for the downgrade trail. The horses tore out their pickets and ran with them, away from the direction of the cottonwood.

The girl was still there, sitting spraddle-legged on the ground, her head rested against the trunk when Wallace and her father got to her. Royer kneeled, pulled her against his chest, saying her name over and over. A hiccup erupted from her. She giggled.

"I am so drunk . . . so drunk . . . I can't stand . . ."

Royer's voice shook. "Don't try, baby. Lie down and sleep. What did you and Rojas talk about to make him leave you alone?"

She giggled again, rolled her head against his chest. Her voice came muffled. "I told him he could kiss me, after he had . . . but if he did anything more he wouldn't get his ransom. I said no American man would pay a cent for a woman who had been used that way. She would be disgraced. He said he had patience, he would wait until you brought much money, then he would show me a real man."

Without warning she was limp, sound asleep. Wallace went for the serape, covered her where her father had lowered her, then the men lay down, drained by the night.

They slept late. The day was hot before they roused. There was still food at the embers of the bandit fire. They wolfed it cold, then walked, carrying three saddles, canteens, armed with the outlaws' weapons. There was no use going back to bury Bo Short. He would have been trampled into red mud and scavenging animals would by now have carried that away.

The horses had not run far. Collecting them all Wallace and Royer went back to lash the bodies across six animals. Pat rode on, finding cattle in small clusters and had almost all of them in a gather when the men got there. Chihuahua lay only one more day ahead. There they took the bodies to a grateful *jefe* and sold the herd for the small price offered. Royer visited Father Louis to tell him the country was rid of Pedro Rojas. While Wallace and Pat waited for him on the street the girl said thoughtfully, "My uncle's ranch could be rebuilt. It could be beautiful again, a fine place. If someone . . . you perhaps . . . would want to stay."

Dork Wallace was tempted. A ranch of his own was the stuff of dreams. But this girl would not be there. He could not ask her now to marry him, to stay in Mexico. That smacked too much of Lida Grant's deceit, as though he were asking only for the property. Further, possession of Twin R was not yet established. Phil Royer might legally own it but old Frank Pease could be counted on not to give it up without some sort of trouble.

He said with a wry smile, "Not yet, anyway. Let's go on home . . . To Texas."

CHAPTER
FOURTEEN

Frank Ace Pease was hugely satisfied. Phil Royer and Dork Wallace were gone where they would cause him no more trouble, his wife was buried and could never reappear to make any claims on him. He was also amused. Bucko Sollars' gang was crewing Twin R, hanging around hoping Royer and Wallace would show up again so they could collect the rewards Pease had let stand. Royer's old bunch had scattered, would not hire out to Pease, and he needed men on his new spread.

Sollars was driving the buckboard into Del Rio with Pease beside him, and the rancher's horse tied on behind, to restock the depleted Twin R storehouse. The one thing that galled the old man was the gluttonous way Bucko's crowd went through food and he did not trust Sollars to buy on his own supplies that Pease must pay for. But the day was fine and with the hardcases plus his own tough outfit on Lazy P there was no one in all Texas big enough to challenge him.

Heading for Cap Myer's general store the rig passed in front of the courthouse just as three people came out to the steps.

The man in the lead was Phil Royer. Behind him were Dork Wallace and Royer's daughter.

Pease's breath sucked in. Without taking his eyes off the trio he stabbed a bony forefinger against Sollars' thick leg. "The price on them don't hold now. I got the ranch, so their hides ain't worth paying for."

"Hell of a thing," Sollars growled. "Why didn't you say so two weeks ago? I think I better collect for not blowing off your head."

Phil Royer had lifted a hand to stop the wagon, dropped lightly down the steps, and was crossing the sidewalk, calling pleasantly.

"Hello, Frank. You're just the man I want to see."

The easy manner was a shock to Pease. He had expected never to see this man again, but should they meet there ought to be outrage. In a guarded tone he said, "Where you been?"

"Mexico." Phil Royer smiled. "Bucko, are you still gunning for Dork and me?"

"Naw." Sollars sounded disgusted. "This cheapskate called it off."

"Glad to hear that. Ace, how are you enjoying married life?"

The old rancher put on a mournful face and a grieving tone. "Poor little Annie got herself killed."

"Oh?" Royer was genuinely shocked. "I'm sorry to hear that. What happened?"

"Stage she was on was held up. She tried to save her money and was shot."

Lida Grant's death did not deeply affect Royer but the mention of money made him curious.

"How much was she carrying?"

"The ten thousand I paid her for Twin R. All of it gone."

Royer stood speechless, studying the little man, incredulous, then asked slowly, "Ace, are you telling me your wife sold the ranch to you?"

Pease squared himself around to face Royer directly, a wicked brightness in the bird eyes. "That's what I just said, ain't it? I got a deed to prove it and you can see it registered right in there." He waggled a victorious finger at the building behind Royer.

There was a long moment through which no one said a word, then a low rumble began deep in Royer's belly, worked up to a chuckle, then exploded into full laughter. Without turning away he waved Pat and Wallace down and when they reached him told them between the erupting bursts, "Ace bought . . . the ranch from . . . the Grant girl. Gave her ten thousand measly dollars . . . that he'll never see again."

Pat Royer's mouth dropped open. She giggled. Dork Wallace raised one eyebrow, put his full attention on Pease and Bucko Sollars, his hand hovering near his belt.

Royer said, "Ace, that's beautiful. Hoodwinked by a slip of a girl. That deed isn't worth the paper and ink."

Frank Pease turned lobster red and shrieked. "Like hell it ain't. Spang Cooper wrote it out and witnessed it when Annie signed it. I saw her sign it."

Phil Royer's smile was wide. "You saw Lida Grant sign it. Ann Royer was killed with her family in Mexico."

"You're plumb crazy. It's another trick to grab for Twin R again but it won't work. I paid good money for that place and everything on it, and what I buy I keep."

Wagging his head like a metronome Royer drew a paper from a pocket, unfolded it, and put it in Pease's hand.

"Here's Judge Bow's order dispossessing you because your title isn't valid. He issued it when I gave him a letter from the priest who buried Ann and her parents. The *jefe* of Chihuahua notarized that. Twin R is mine, Frank, and you have until tomorrow to clear off it."

Pease blustered, scrambling to the sidewalk, snarling. "I want a look at that letter. I don't believe any such thing."

They watched him scamper up the steps like a spider on a hot stick toward Judge Bow's chambers. Sollars looked after him, an ugly twist at the corner of his mouth. Pat Royer sighed, tired from the long ride north.

"I'm going to the hotel, clean up and rest until suppertime . . . and just relish this picture of Frank Pease." She crossed the street, smiling at everyone she passed.

Phil Royer said, "A bath sounds good to me, and a shave and haircut."

Dork Wallace told him, "A drink to celebrate first? Then I'll join you at the barbershop."

They had turned in at the Mermaid before Frank Pease came out of the courthouse looking like a dog

154

with a bone caught in its throat. He climbed up beside Sollars, snorting through his nose.

"Damn little bitch really levered me."

"She didn't live to spend any of it."

"That don't do me no good. My money's gone and I lose the ranch. But by damn I'll have the cattle."

Sollars cawed. "You think Royer's going to give them to you?"

"We're going to take them. Drive them over the river, sell them below the line. Any of the big haciendas will take them. I've done a lot of business down there."

"So have I. They don't care what brand a cow's wearing. But what are Royer and Wallace going to be doing while we round them up?"

Pease grunted. "What can they do? The old crew's busted up and gone and tough as Dork is he's only one man."

Sollars spat. "And not so tough. I can take him any time he tries to pull a gun."

Frank Pease had reservations on that score. He had trained Wallace, seen him develop over the years, but a warning could ruin this last chance to recover any of the ten thousand lost dollars.

He said instead, "So ride out there tonight and start the gather at daybreak. It's less than a month since the main roundup and they should still be pretty well bunched. Shove them south. I got to go home and see the boys there are doing their job and I'll send somebody ahead of you to Don Miguel Torres. He'll have a crew meet you across the river. I'll be there as soon as you are to collect. Anything over my ten

155

thousand is yours. Before you leave town we'll pick up grub enough for the drive but we'll forget the storehouse."

Sollars drove on to the store and sat on the wagon thinking while Frank Pease went in with his list. The rancher came out and without waiting to see the order loaded got on his horse and rode for Lazy P. When Myer brought the sacks and tossed them aboard Sollars turned back to the livery instead of starting for Twin R at once. There was plenty of time and Bucko felt that he thought better in a bar.

If Frank Pease was not going on the drive the opportunity was open for Sollars to make the biggest strike of his career. Twin R and Lazy P had a long common border. The men who followed him were enough to take the Royer stock to Mexico. But if he could find enough more to ride for him they could sweep up a good number of Pease's own animals, hurry a double herd south and old Miguel Torres would have them all scattered over his miles before Frank Pease came down. On top of that Sollars could collect for all the cows and be long gone with everything they brought. Pease would be alone or nearly so, and like Dork Wallace he had no way to stop Bucko's boys.

A supper and a bottle of whiskey later he had it all figured out except where to find the extra hands. Then that solved itself for him.

About eight o'clock in the evening a group rode up Main Street yelling and firing, come, it sounded, for a night on the town. Bucko Sollars shoved away from the bar, went to look over the louvered doors, then flapped

156

out to the sidewalk, waving the riders down. If he had scoured Texas he could not have found six men better for his purpose.

The Raffertys, what was left of the tribe. Old Jonas, his three sons still alive, Ned, Jake, and Luke, and two nephews, Buster and Steve. Two other sons, Clem and Rafe, had been killed the night Sollars first jumped the Pease crew on Twin R, but that could be explained away if Bucko could make Jonas listen. He was not afraid they would shoot him here on the street for over the louvers he had seen Monk Hobart paused on the corner watching the arrival and the Raffertys walked wide of the night marshal.

He called. "Light boys. I'll buy a drink."

Jonas Rafferty glanced at Hobart, then thrust out his lantern jaw. "Not with the bastard that got my boys killed, I don't drink."

The big outlaw walked closer, keeping his voice down. "Wasn't me. Look to Dork Wallace and Ace Pease for that. I've got an offer to make you so get down and come in."

Rafferty sat very still, saying nothing; a hardscrabble rancher with a little outfit that barely supported the family, he ruled as a tyrant.

Sollars added, "Good money in it for you."

Jonas still hesitated, then shrugged, and stepped down. "I'll listen. You boys set here and wait."

He went into the saloon on Sollars' heels, crowded to the bar with him, tossed down the drink the bartender poured. "Well?"

Caution came late to Bucko Sollars. The room was too full of ears. He picked up the bottle, spun a coin on the counter, waved Rafferty with him again. On the sidewalk they drank again from the neck, then left the bottle with the horsemen and walked to the middle of the dust ribbon. There Sollars made his proposition, adding as a clincher, "You'll never have a better chance to pay off Twin R for your losing two sons. And Jonas, you keep half of what the Lazy P stock brings."

Rafferty stretched a turkey neck toward Sollars, shaking his long head. "We take the risk and do all the work for half? Not enough."

"Two thirds then. I take the rest for the idea."

Sollars would have promised all that Pease's stock was sold for, except that that would have roused suspicion. Once the cattle were in Mexico he would see that the ragtag tribe quietly disappeared, either run off or left dead in the bleak hills. They were a shifty eyed, mangy pack, not to be considered the equals of his own elite band.

"That's better," Jonas said. "When do we start and where?"

"Dawn tomorrow. You pick up the Lazy P stuff that's still close along Devil's Creek and meet us in Carta Valley. We'll all follow the Sycamore to the Rio Grande. There's a good crossing a mile below."

No one on the street showed any curiosity about the conversation. Dork Wallace, at his hotel room window, did. Trail weary as he and the Royers were they had all retired soon after supper, but the Raffertys' noisy arrival had brought Dork bolt upright in the lumpy, sagging bed, then took him padding to the window to see what the gunfire meant. He was in time to look down on Bucko Sollars charging from the saloon to hail the clan, stayed to see him lead Jonas Rafferty inside and waited where he was. That the old man had left the boys mounted suggested that he did not mean to stay in the bar long. When he came out and half-crossed the road with Sollars Dork recognized a conference that was not to be overheard. Suspicion nagged at him that those two should be talking at all and it grew to certainty when Jonas mounted and took his boys out of town at a more deliberate pace than they had come in at. It was a long ride from their distant small ranch for a single drink, and out of doors at that. He watched until Bucko Sollars turned away from the retreating riders and swaggered through the doors again. Then he dressed, strapped on his gun, followed the corridor, and knocked softly at Phil Royer's room, calling his name.

When the sleepy rancher let him in he told him about the street scene. "I don't know what it was about but I think there's more trouble ahead for us."

Royer came sharply awake. "But the court order gives me clear title. What could they do?"

"As vengeful as Frank Pease is and if Sollars is still in with him he could be hiring the Raffertys to burn you out. Or rustle your herd. Or both. I'm going out there now."

Royer spun, reaching for his clothes, saying, "I'll go with you."

"No. Stay in town and hire whoever you can as a crew, then bring them. I'll contact you there as soon as I learn anything."

He left the rancher, took the steps down two at a time, crossed the lobby and stepped out to the porch, then stopped. Bucko Sollars was just coming out of the saloon, a bottle hanging from his hand, turning along the street. Wallace eased back inside, jogged through the dining room and dark kitchen to the rear door. He took the alley parallel to Sollars, pausing at the corners until Bucko passed them and was in the shadows of the livery corral when the man came through the wide front entrance.

The team was still hitched to the buckboard in the runway. Sollars climbed up, drove out, and turned into the road. When he was out of sight Dork Wallace saddled his horse without hurry, wanting to give the wagon enough head start that he could follow undiscovered.

Twin R was all Phil Royer had. The operation was not large enough to keep Wallace's interest. After the enormous herds he had taken up the trail for Frank Pease the few thousand head Royer ran were no challenge, but if they were lost, if Pat's home was destroyed it would break both their hearts.

Wallace trailed Sollars out of Del Rio and as far as the long lane that ran back from the road to Twin R. When the wagon swung into that lane Dork turned aside, detoured through the low rolling hills and rode around him.

CHAPTER
FIFTEEN

Seen from the breast of a mound a quarter mile from the buildings the Twin R headquarters lay at peace beneath the stars that stretched to infinity, looking low enough to be plucked like fruit. There were no lights. Nothing moved.

Dork Wallace tied his horse in the bottom of the depression behind the mound where it could not be seen from the lane or the yard and rolled in his blanket just below the crest. The trip north out of Mexico had been pushed. Bath and shave had refreshed him temporarily but his broken sleep had given him little rest and waves of tiredness shook through his lean body. He slept deeply now, confident that the creak and rumble of the wagon would wake him when Sollars came.

When it did the stars had wheeled. It was nearly four in the morning. Wallace crawled higher until he could look down on the yard. The buckboard passed below the hill and as it approached the buildings Bucko bawled ahead to rouse his crew. Lamps were lit in the bunkhouse and cookshack, the flames growing slowly until yellow light flowed from windows and doors. Men came out to the yard to splash water on their faces at the wash bench. Sollars got down and walked to them and there was a lengthy talk.

Smoke rose from the fresh-fed cook fire and shortly the smells of coffee and frying meat came up to Wallace, making him aware of hunger. In his concern and hurry to be here he had not thought of a grub sack. It was too late now. He would have to do without food for he could not guess how long.

He lay with his rifle at his side while the men ate. Sollars would not start his mischief on an empty belly. But if it was a burnout he had in mind Dork was ready to shoot anyone who tried to start a blaze. From his hilltop his gun could reach the lot of them.

The eastern sky was light when they appeared again, showing the figures clearly. They set no fires. Some went to the corral to saddle, others dragged the chuck wagon from the shed and brought a team while the cook moved the new supplies from the buckboard to the trail kitchen. They might be simply getting ready to move out as Royer had ordered and taking the loaded chuck wagon would be typical of Bucko Sollars, but Dork Wallace did not believe this was so innocent an activity.

With full daylight the cook took the wagon out, toward the north, then the crew mounted and spurred ahead of him. It had all the looks of a trail drive and it would not take long to strip this range. In a few days the whole herd could be in Mexico and dispersed through half of Chihuahua.

Dork Wallace searched his mind for a way they could be stopped. There were no neighboring ranchers who would stand up against Frank Pease, he knew that from long experience, and he felt certain this was a Lazy P action. The nearest sheriff had only two deputies. Rangers from Austin could not be reached and brought in time. Phil Royer would be trying to pick up men but at this season, after roundup, any good, reliable riders who did not work for a local brand would be away, trailing the herds to market. Only the shiftless and the drifters would still be in Del Rio, more apt to throw in with the raiders than to fight them. Whatever could be done would be up to Royer himself and Wallace, with only one faint chance of help, and he would have to make sure his guess was right before he asked for that.

When Sollars' people were well out of sight Wallace got up, stiff from the long watch, went down for his horse and rode in to the ranch. There was still fire in the big range and half a pot of coffee on it, warm. Dork's stomach growled as he poured a cup and drank while he looked for food. The larder had been cleaned out. Only a few leftover biscuits were still on the long table. Nothing had been cleaned up and there was a half inch of grease in the fry pan. Wallace split the biscuits and soaked them in the grease, then cut down the ham bone that hung from the rafter for the scrap of meat at the string end. Poor fare and little of it but it would hold him for a while.

When he had eaten it all he went to the main house, found paper and a pencil in Royer's office, and wrote a note telling what he had seen and what he proposed, and asked that a messenger be sent to Austin as a last resort.

163

Afterward he walked out to the horse. It was leg weary from the Mexican trail but the corral was empty, there was no fresh animal to change to. He remembered how often during a roundup he had ridden four horses to their limit without stopping to rest himself for the Lazy P. Out of loyalty to the ranch. Such loyalty made a forty-dollar-a-month hand work and fight and sometimes die for the brand that hired him. But he owed nothing more to Frank Pease. It was Phil Royer, or, more honestly, Pat, for whom he would go to such ends, nurse this mount along until he could find another and do all he could to prevent loss of the herd.

He rode north after Sollars, slow and watchful. If they were combing the brush for cows they could be anywhere and he did not want a surprise meeting. But it was more likely they would begin in the area of the last roundup, miles above the headquarters.

In midafternoon he smelled a campfire and went on with even more caution. The land had roughened into gullies and ridges with thick brush. It made good cover. He climbed each rise on foot, to spare the horse and to survey what lay beyond before he crossed. One high point proved the last in that series and from there he had a sweeping view across broken country, saw the chuck wagon at a distance and tied his animal to watch from there. Cattle grazed in small groups. He could spot their movement from the elevation but in the dense brush they would be hard to comb out.

Beyond the wagon one bunch appeared, driven by two riders who hazed them into a rough corral where

164

calves had been held a month ago for branding by the different owners. The work went on until evening, men in pairs going and coming, pausing for coffee, then riding after more stock. By the time they quit there were five to six hundred crowded within the enclosure.

At dark they straggled in. Eight men. That meant the Raffertys were not working from this wagon. If indeed they were working with Sollars it was from some camp of their own and no telling where.

His horse had had some hours' rest. At full dark Wallace mounted, turned back down the ridge, and angled toward the Lazy P. His old crew should be there and Bent Bentley was as honest a man as Frank Pease had let him be. If this brazen rustling was put to him he might quit Pease and bring the boys to ride for Royer, and with them at his back he would have a more than fair chance against Bucko Sollars' brute gang. After that the Raffertys would be easy to chase off the range.

Within five miles he crossed the Devil's Creek boundary. Six miles into Lazy P a small fire winked. Dork rode toward that with full caution. It should be some of Pease's crew, but it was odd to find them so far from headquarters at night this time of year when there was little but line riding to be done. And whoever this was he was well inside Lazy P. He thought of Jonas Rafferty and his boys and drew a long breath. Was Sollars double-crossing Frank Pease, reaching for what they could grab of his cattle as well as Phil Royer's? The idea had a sardonic humor if that was what the fire meant.

Dork Wallace was not the only curious rider heading for the little light. Bent Bentley had been in this area that afternoon, had spotted distant riders rounding up a clutch of cows, and known they were not his men. One animal he identified, an old mulley cow with a broken horn. A good hand with a herd Bentley had the usual cowboy's opinion of rustlers. He had ridden hell bent for Lazy P and told Frank Pease what he had seen. Pease had blown sky high.

"On my range? My stock? That damned Sollars . . ."

"I don't think so. I'm pretty sure one was Jonas Rafferty. You know how he rides, like a buzzard taking off with his elbows stuck straight out from his sides."

Pease turned the air blue. It did not occur to him that Raffertys working on his cows would be tied in with Bucko Sollars. He figured they were raiding on their own. The rest of his crew had gone to Del Rio excepting the messenger on his way to Mexico, but this had to be taken care of immediately. He yelled at Bentley.

"Get a scatter gun while I saddle up. We'll hang those thieving bastards."

Bent Bentley said sourly, "There's at least six of them. Is Sollars still on Twin R? I'd better go bring his crowd."

Frank Pease had told no one about Bucko Sollars' present project and he did not want Bentley anywhere near the place to see the gather.

"Rafferty will be long gone before Bucko could get there. Do like I say. We can take them ourselves."

Bentley was not enthusiastic, but he was drawing a hundred a month as foreman and he wanted to keep the job. Muttering, he went for the shotgun and filled his pockets with buckshot shells.

Three hours later they approached the Rafferty camp. Tired from the long day of fighting cows and brush the tribe was asleep except the nephews Buster and Steve, who slowly circled the restless herd as night riders. Pease and Bentley let the near man pass, then quietly followed him, drawing close behind him. Buster Rafferty sat slack in his saddle, half asleep, keeping his seat by instinct. As the Lazy P men rode in on either side and eased guns into his ribs he came awake, gasping.

Frank Pease told Bentley, "Lift his gun, then throw a rope around him and tie him to that tree while I catch the other."

The foreman dropped a noose over Buster's head, dragged him off the horse, towed him strangling to the cottonwood and bound him there so he could not move, could barely breathe. He was still working with the rope when Steve rode by. Frank Pease did not wait for help. He jammed his gun in the drowsing man's chest, saying, "Reach."

The boy was young, not bright. His reaction was a shocked yell that brought the Raffertys at the camp rolling to their feet. Pease did not shoot him. He wanted all of them to hang, to die slowly. He raked his barrel down the side of the head, knocked Steve off the horse. The boy was stunned but not out, and in falling he grabbed blindly for something to hold to. What he

167

caught was the stock of the rifle in the scabbard under Frank Pease's knee. It dragged out and down, the barrel swinging wildly, the gun exploding as Steve's finger convulsed on the trigger. Then he was on the ground, knocked cold by the fall. The horse bolted away.

Lead flew across the herd but there was too much distance for it to be much danger. Unaware that Bentley was not with him Frank Pease rode against the cows firing, shouting, waving his hat. They bawled, lunging up in fright. Stampedes had been started by animals that saw nothing more dreadful than lightning and this bunch was no exception. A black three-year-old started the run and in seconds the whole gather was charging. Directly toward the Rafferty camp, with Frank Pease hurrahing them.

The men scattered out of the way. All but Jonas' eldest son Luke made it to safety. He was overrun and trampled into a bloody mass. Jonas caught one of the night riders' saddled horses as it dashed past, held it until the cattle had thundered into the night, then mounted. He sat a long moment looking down on Luke's torn body, lifted the rifle from the boot and rode deliberately at where Frank Pease sat watching the stunned group.

Left with only his short gun Pease waited for the rider's approach. When he was near enough he sent a slug that caught Jonas in the leg, but the man kept coming as he stalked the old rancher. Pease fired again and again, certain that every shot hit home. Still Jonas rode at him.

He yelled. "Bentley. For God sake shoot him."

There was no answer. Swinging his horse Pease discovered the foreman far behind him, lying on the ground where Steve's accidental shot had knocked him. He panicked. How could you fight a man who would not fall? He dug in his spurs to turn and the horse jumped. Jonas brought his rifle up with slow care and fired once. It was enough. Struck in the middle of his back Pease threw up his arms and pitched sideways. One foot caught in the stirrup and the horse dragged the dead body until it stopped where Bent Bentley's animal stood shaking.

Jonas was still in his saddle, a hunched figure watching the running horse. Then he turned and rode back to the ruined camp. He sat above his son's remains a moment longer, then collapsed to the ground, dead by the time his last boys reached him.

From the hillside he had been descending Dork Wallace saw it all. He stayed there until Jonas was tied across the horse, the night rider tied to the tree was freed and the unconscious one roused and the clan rode out, whether to join Sollars or go home he did not know. When they had gone he rode down, found Frank Pease dead and Bentley groaning, just sitting up, pressing a handkerchief against the bleeding graze along his scalp. While the foreman recovered Dork lifted the rancher's bantam body across his saddle, roped him there, and helped Bentley to mount. They rode in silence most of the way. Finally Bentley grunted.

169

"The damned old fool, thinking he could jump that clan with just the two of us. He was crazy."

"Yep. But he was hell on wheels." Wallace still had to admire the fierce old fighter. "And you're out of a job. You want another? I'll hire the whole crew if you'll take on Bucko Sollars' gang. They're stripping Twin R and I think Rafferty had thrown in with him to add a Lazy P herd to a drive to Mexico. Did Frank tell you the girl he married was a phony, that Phil Royer still owns his ranch?"

"The hell." Bentley found a laugh. "I like that. I never did hold with Ace's shenanigans. Sure, I'd love a crack at Sollars if he's rustling."

At dawn they rousted the Lazy P crew out, heavy-eyed from a late night in town. They buried Frank Pease beside his wife, wondering aloud who would buy in the beautiful ranch at a public auction, since the old man had no relatives. Dork Wallace ached to own it, but the few dollars he had saved were many thousands short of what it would bring.

Over breakfast he made his offer of jobs again and was taken up without hesitation as if they were all anxious, more comfortable with the idea of riding under him again.

He laid out the strategy they would follow. They would not rush in but wait until Sollars had gathered what cattle he could and started them toward the river. That would avoid a bloody fight with the entire gang. But during the drive they would be strung along the column where they could be hit one or two at a time and should not take any losses themselves. They stayed at the headquarters that day making up the rest they needed for a long ride and getting their trail gear ready. Only two would be left there to watch over the ranch until officialdom claimed it for sale.

CHAPTER
SIXTEEN

A little after daylight what was left of the Raffertys trailed into Bucko Sollars' camp on Twin R with the bodies. Bucko listened to their story, unaffected by these deaths but delighted when they said Frank Pease and Bent Bentley had also fallen.

"Best break we could have," he cawed. "We'll move what we've got here down the trail, then come back and clean out Lazy P. You go on over there and start shoving the old coot's cows this way so they'll be ready when we want them."

The oldest surviving Rafferty son rode with his shoulders dropped. He shook his head. "We ain't going to do that, Bucko, with Paw and Luke both gone. Long as they was around to tell us what to do we did it, but Ned and Jake ain't right in the head to know what's what and I don't want no trouble with rangers. You ain't got no ranch, no cows to worry about but I'm different. Our place ain't fancy but I don't aim to try anything that could make me lose it."

Sollars spat in disgust and turned his back. When the Raffertys had moved on he went to the fire where his gang was breakfasting, in a fever now to be moving, and ordered the chuck wagon started for Mexico as soon as it could be readied, the cattle driven out of the corral and headed for the border. With the Lazy P abandoned he could clean it out with his own people right after these animals were delivered to Don Torres.

They pushed them hard all that day and the next and on the second evening camped just short of the pass into Carta Valley. Once beyond that bottleneck it was all down grade to the best crossing in fifty miles, and there was no one to interfere.

The pass crossed a ridge, steep and narrow, half a mile long. In the morning Sollars' crowd began driving the cattle through the slot, six hundred brutes bawling at the fast pace, long horns clattering against each other as they tossed their heads in protest at being jammed together, strung out in a long thin line between the near vertical walls.

From the rocky tops on both sides Dork Wallace's old Lazy P crew looked down through the churned dust. Half were stationed at the far end of the cut to wait until the point riders came below them, the rest at the entrance Sollars would drive into. Dork saw two point men lead the first animals up the grade, a tight smile on his lips. Neither of them was Bucko Sollars and it was Sollars he wanted. So Bucko would be at the rear, probably with the extra horses where he could see that no cows strayed.

The timing was going to be close. If the herd was strung out too long its head could be through the pass before the men riding drag entered it, and firing at the two on point would warn those behind, spoil the ambush.

As he watched Dork Wallace frowned in surprise and disapproval. There were Sollars' men spaced in among the cattle, yipping, urging them on dangerously fast. In the narrow confine they would be in trouble if the animals bolted. Three of them passed below him before the drag appeared and started through. There were another three there behind the cows, pushing them. Then he located Bucko, as he expected, with another man keeping the horse herd bunched, still outside the walls.

At that moment there was firing at the head of the column, more than should be needed. He judged that one or both of the point riders had been missed as they left the pass, but that was not too important. He heard other guns along the rims taking out the riders among the cows. Predictably the animals stampeded up the trail. Wallace hoped for their sakes the riders had died by lead rather than sharp, pounding hoofs, but there was little time to think of that.

At the first rattle of gunfire Bucko Sollars had abandoned the horses, spurred to join the drag riders and with them began shooting up at the rocks toward the puffs of smoke that pinpointed Wallace's men. Beside Dork Bent Bentley cut down the two nearest men, wounded a third so that he dropped off his horse and dived for cover.

Bucko Sollars reared his animal, hauled it around, and drove back out of range.

"Take over," Wallace told Bentley. "When it's finished here take the boys through and bring the herd back. I'm going after Bucko."

Running, jumping, Wallace dropped back of the ridge to where the crew had tied their horses. He made his saddle without touching the stirrup and wheeled down to the trail. Sollars was ahead, already with a half mile lead that increased with every running stride. The big bay the outlaw rode was deep-chested, strong, fresh. Wallace's animal had carried him through the night. He would not catch the man by running his mount to death.

He dropped to a walk. It would likely be a long chase, but Bucko's horse left plain tracks to follow. They crossed the valley and by afternoon wound into the row of low, rounded hills that bounded this side of the Twin R. Sollars was heading for the Royer ranch.

Wallace's jaw bunched. Pat and Phil were probably there by now with whatever scrub crew Royer had picked up, but none of them would be a match for the giant outlaw.

Sollars was in and out of sight, alternately running and walking the bay, keeping his lead but no longer adding to it, saving his horse too. Wallace began driving hard whenever he could not see Bucko, but he was still three quarters of a mile behind when Sollars reached the yard. By the time Dork got there the bay stood blowing, head drooped low, tied to the porch rail. He did not see the big man nor anyone else. He jumped from the saddle, running in, drawing his gun. Then, before he reached the steps the front door slammed open, Sollars shoved Pat Royer out ahead of him, one arm around her neck, turning half around to show the other hand holding a gun against her spine. Dork skidded to a stop. Sollars grinned, shouting, "Right where you are, Wallace. Throw your iron over here."

Wallace groaned and tossed the short gun forward, looking toward the sides of the house. Sollars laughed.

"There's just us here, cowboy. No use looking for help."

He prodded the girl to the porch railing, crowded her against it, then in a sudden move swung his gun away from her and put a heavy slug through the head of Dork Wallace's horse to put him afoot. The only animal Dork had seen as he passed the corral was Pat's small mare that could not overtake the big bay even winded as it was.

But even as the explosion came Pat twisted, caught Sollars' wrist in both hands, threw herself to the side. It dragged Sollars off balance, his foot tripped on her leg and he fell to his knees, the grip on her neck broken.

"Dork . . . Dork . . ."

Wallace did not need the call. He vaulted the porch rail, swinging a boot as he landed, the toe under Sollars' wide chin snapping the head back. The gun flipped out of his hand, clattered to the floor. Wallace scooped for it but it was out of reach. As he dived toward it Sollars rolled, clubbing a fist against the back of Dork's neck, stunning him. In that moment the huge outlaw shoved to his feet, clubbed again at Wallace's jaw, sprawled him on the boards.

Bucko swung away, looking for his gun. It wasn't on the floor. It was in Pat Royer's steady hand. He grabbed at it with his left hand. She shot him in that shoulder. The bullet did not stop him. He jumped for her. To

176

keep him from having it she threw the gun to the yard. Sollars back-handed her across the face and as she fell jumped for the rail.

Wallace landed on his back, driving them both to the floor in a tangle. Even shot in the shoulder Sollars was more than a match for Wallace. Dork knew he would have to win this fight quickly or be killed viciously, for Bucko was an animal whose pleasure was brutality. Sollars was on his face, Wallace astride him, his knees clamped tight. With both fists he battered at the shoulder, hearing Sollars' yells, then he locked his fingers together, put all his strength in a rabbit punch on the thick neck. Sollars went limp. Wallace twisted off him but the sagging did not last. Bucko was losing blood. It smeared the boards and his hands slipped in it as he pushed himself up. Wallace had to wait, to fill his exhausted lungs, and as he gasped Sollars got to his feet, unsteady, stumbled to the porch post at the edge of the steps, leaning against it.

Then in a surprise move Sollars ran down to the yard. Wallace thought Bucko was through, like most bullies a coward when he was losing. It was almost too late when he saw his mistake. Sollars was after the gun Wallace had thrown at the bottom of the steps, was stooped for it when Dork leaped, both feet in Bucko's back driving him face down again. That knocked all Sollars' wind out. While he sucked for air Wallace caught up the gun, spun, and got the one Pat had tossed in the grass, then faced Sollars, out of reach of a new lunge, both barrels trained on the prone man.

Sollars rolled, breathing hard, looking into the guns. When he could manage it he sat up, his eyes showing confidence that Wallace would not shoot him, finally got to his feet, reached for the hat that had fallen at the edge of the porch, adjusted the crease and settled it on his head. He even smiled.

"Well, cowboy, what do we do now?"

Wallace told him quietly, "We lock you in the blacksmith shop until the crew comes. Then we take you to Del Rio for the sheriff to hold for the Rangers. There's enough blood on your hands now to earn you a hanging."

Sollars' eyes changed. He was going to jump, to go down under the gun rather than a rope. Dork Wallace saw it.

"Don't try it, Bucko. I can shoot both legs out from under you. I don't want to kill you but I will if that's the only way to stop you."

The big man flapped his hands out from his sides, then let them drop. He turned toward the blacksmith shop. Wallace followed out of reach of any further try, holstering one gun when the man walked inside to close the thick door and set the iron bar in the brackets. Sollars could shake the door all he wanted to but the prongs hanging from the bar would keep it from being jarred free. There were no windows in the shop. Light was only needed when the forge was being used and then the door must be open anyway. Bucko Sollars could not be held in any more secure cell.

Pat Royer stood on the porch until Wallace returned. There was a red swelling where Sollars had slapped her

178

and he saw a tension in her body when he came up before her, stopping at the top step, asking, "Did he hurt you badly?"

She lifted the light gray eyes to him, open and inviting, then when he made no closer move they slowly closed, her body sagged, giving at the knees. In one quick stride he caught her as she fell. She lay limp across his arm, her head back exposing her firm, tanned throat, her hands hanging behind her.

His own throat constricted with a rush of emotion. He lifted her as he would a child, carried her indoors, and laid her on the long, cowhide-covered couch in the parlor. Her breathing was shallow and rapid, throbbing in the hollow at the base of her neck. Wallace chafed her hands, her cheeks for some moments before the eyes opened on him again, and she smiled.

Dork kissed her impulsively, hard, holding her lips when she responded. When he would raise his head her arm went around his shoulders, keeping him against her. Finally he shoved up roughly.

"I had no right . . . Your fainting . . ."

Her smile widened with mischief. "God helps those who help themselves, Dork. It took you long enough."

He looked startled, then shook his head. "I haven't anything to offer you. Just a foreman's wages. I wish I could give you the Lazy P, something worthy of you, but it's crazy even to think of it."

She reached for his hands, pressed them against her ribs, laughing now. "It isn't crazy to think of the ranch in Mexico."

"That isn't mine either, Pat."

"It's ours. I asked Phil to give it to us before we got back to Texas. He said he would as soon as I could make you speak."

A deep flush burned his face. "You knew how I felt that long ago?"

"I knew. Phil did too. He bet me the ranch you wouldn't say anything unless I forced you to."

He bent to kiss her more fiercely, to lift her to his lap, did not hear Phil Royer tramp into the room until he coughed and said in exaggerated dismay, "I just can't win for losing. Not only my daughter but a ranch and the best foreman Twin R ever had."